I0714040

Other historical fiction books by Sherry A. Burton

*The Orphan Train Saga**
Discovery (book one)
Shameless (book two)
Treachery (book three)
Guardian (book four)

** A note from the author regarding The Orphan Train Saga. While each book tells a different child's story, some of the children's lives intertwine. For that reason, I recommend reading the books in order so that you avoid spoilers.*

Ezra's Story
The Orphan Train Extras

Written by Sherry A. Burton

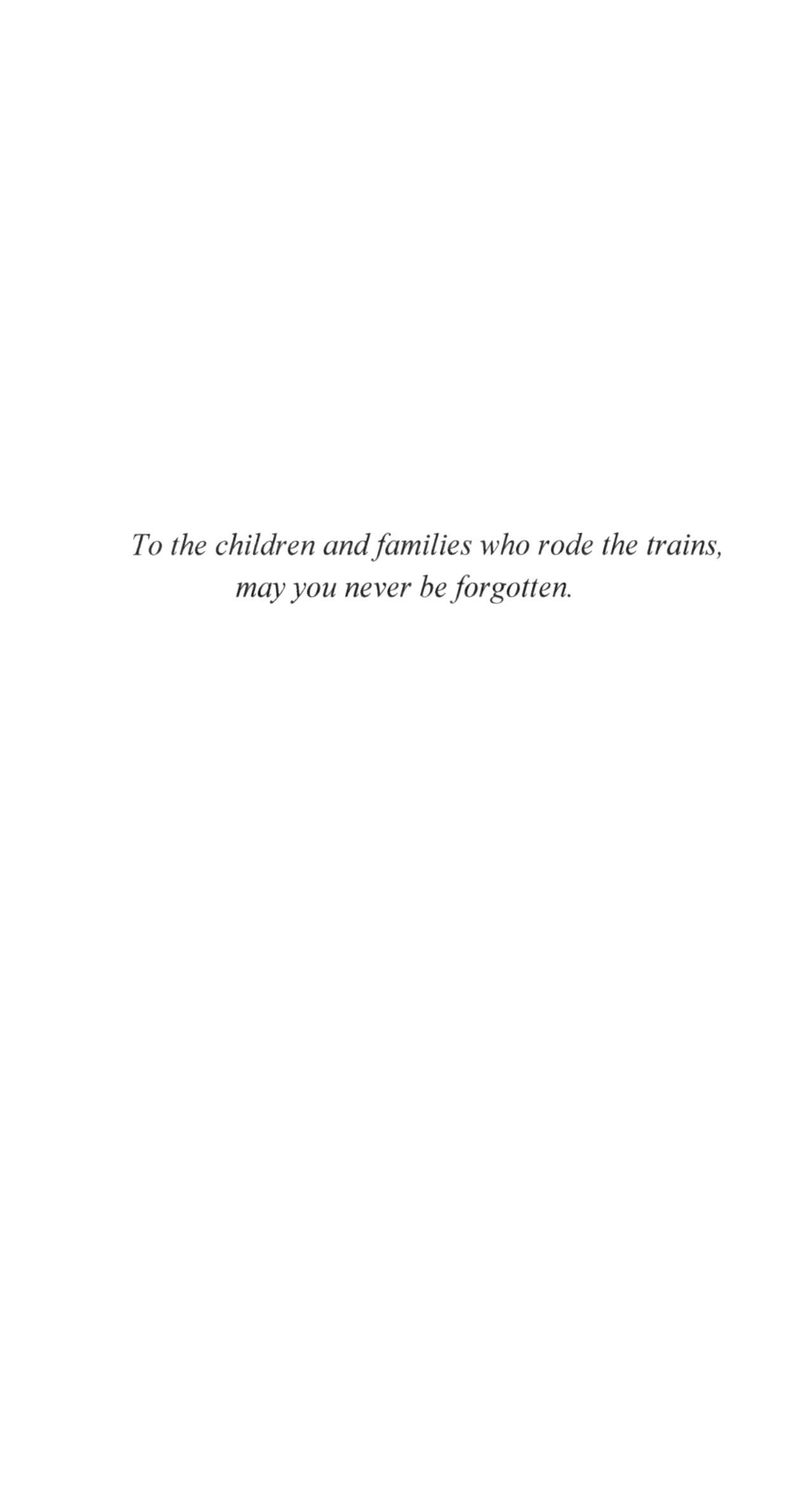

*To the children and families who rode the trains,
may you never be forgotten.*

Table of Contents

Chapter One

May, 1915

Ezra sat on the window sill in the front room of the family's apartment watching as the sun inched over the rooftops of the nearby buildings. The beams of light added a welcoming glow to the dark room, suggesting the promise of a bright new day. He always clung to that hope until around suppertime, when Papa would arrive home with his clothes smelling of stale cigars, his skin leaching the stench of liquor, which seeped from his pores in bubbles of sweat. Ezra hated that smell and loathed the darkness that was sure to follow. His papa was a monster in a man's body, quick to anger and ruling with a heavy hand. It hadn't always been that way. He used to enjoy spending time with his papa. However, things had changed and seemed to be getting gradually worse of late.

Ezra blamed his sister, Anastasia. Anna, as she preferred to be called, had taken him and his younger brother, Tobias, to the market one day and had vanished seemingly into thin air, leaving him and Tobias to explain why she hadn't returned home. Not that they'd had much to tell. One minute, she was at the applecart teaching both boys how to steal apples, and the next, she was gone. Even though he and Tobias left out the part about stealing apples, Papa had been furious. His momma tried to soothe Papa's fury and in return had taken the brunt of his anger. Later, when Papa wasn't around, Ezra asked her why she hadn't cried upon hearing the news of his sister's disappearance. His mother merely shushed him, telling him not to mention Anna again, especially if Papa was in the room. A year had passed since his sister disappeared, and in that time, no one dared say her name. He sometimes tried to remember what she looked like, only recalling that she had dark flowing hair and looked a lot like their mother, except for a thin scar that stretched the length of her face. If not for a coat hanging in the closet of Tobias' bedroom, a room that once belonged to Anna, he would have wondered if he'd only dreamed of his sister's existence. He was angry with her for leaving, but mostly, he was angry she hadn't taken him and his brother with her.

Unable to sleep, Ezra waited for his papa to rise, hoping to catch him before he left for the day, aiming to tell him he didn't like the way he was treating Momma. Even though he was only seven, he knew it best to speak to his father in the wee hours of the morning while he was still in his right mind. Once his father dove into the bottle, there would be no reasoning with the man.

The door to his parents' bedroom opened and Papa emerged, work boots in hand. He always began the day looking put together, hair neatly combed, and his clothes, though worn, were clean, thanks to Momma. Still, they hung on him, and even in the dim lighting, the man appeared thin and haggard. Momma often told Ezra he was the spitting image of the man. She'd smile when saying it, as if it was something for him to be proud of. Ezra wasn't impressed. He wasn't so sure he wanted to look like a monster. Granted, the man in front of him didn't look so fearful at the moment, but Ezra had witnessed it enough to know the monster was in there, waiting to be set free.

Papa looked up, saw him sitting on the windowsill, and pulled a chair close. "You're up early," he said, stuffing his foot into a boot.

It's difficult to sleep when my stomach is empty. Keeping the thought to himself, Ezra shrugged. "Couldn't sleep."

"Children should not have trouble sleeping," his father said as he bent to lace his boots.

Ezra thought to tell him that no one could sleep with all the yelling and screaming behind his parents' bedroom door, then decided against it. Instead, he opted for a different approach.

"Don't leave."

His father finished looping the lace and pulled it firm before straightening. "I'm going to work."

Liar. "You don't work. You go to the bar and drink until time to come home, and when you come home, you're mean."

His father narrowed his eyes. "You keeping tabs on me, boy?"

Ezra's mouth went dry and he worked to swallow his fear. "I heard you and Momma fighting. You go down to the dock, but you don't work. You wait 'til the bar opens and you sit in there gambling and drinking until time to come home for dinner."

"What I do is none of your concern." His father's voice was surprisingly calm.

Ezra pulled himself taller and gathered his courage. "You make Momma cry. That's my concern."

"Your mother should be ashamed of herself, putting you up to this," Papa said, glancing toward the bedroom where Ezra's mother slept.

"Momma doesn't know. She's never spoken badly about you, not even when you're mean to her. She says it's not your fault that you have a sickness. But you ain't sick. You just drink too much."

His father closed his eyes for a moment, then opened them once more. When he spoke, Ezra saw the man behind the monster. "You don't know what it's like, son."

"I know some. Like you ain't mean right now, but if you leave, then come home, you'll be mean. So don't leave."

"I'm afraid it's not that easy. Once the drink's got you, there's no stopping it. If I were to stay, I'd eventually go to the cabinet where I keep my bottle." He heaved a heavy sigh then stood to leave. "I'm afraid the devil's got my soul."

Ezra waited until his father neared the door before responding. "Then don't come back."

His father hesitated briefly before leaving without another word.

Ezra waited for him to return. When he didn't, he went back to his bed and closed his eyes. Sometimes it was easier sleeping knowing the monster that claimed to be his father was gone.

***

Ezra sat on the floor next to Tobias, who was contentedly lining up marbles and rolling them along the hard floor like a snake. Now and then, one would break free and five-year-old Tobias would scamper to his knees, chasing it across the floor.

His mother stood at the kitchen stove, hair pulled high, showing deep worry lines that etched her face. He watched as she painstakingly peeled the smallest slivers of skin from two potatoes and, slicing them into small cubes, placed them into the cast-iron skillet. She dipped a cup into the cornmeal and put the contents into a bowl. His mouth watered as she added a teaspoon of sugar and a sprinkle of salt, then poured boiling water into the bowl before mixing everything together. He'd seen her do it often enough to know there would be johnnycakes served with dinner. She set the mixture aside then stirred the small pan of beans that bubbled on the stove. Using her apron to hold the skillet's handle, she shifted the potatoes, then wiped her forehead with the same grease-stained apron. His mother had grown exceedingly thin over the last few months, her dark hair had lost its luster, and her face looked pale and drawn. Something was terribly wrong, as just this morning, he'd heard her getting sick in the washroom. He'd wanted to ask her how she could throw up when she had nothing in her stomach to lose, but she'd given him a stern look when he approached, so he'd let the question go unasked.

His mother surveyed the stove, a frown flitting across her face as she studied the meager offerings. Instantly, he knew she would not be eating supper again this night.

Ezra tried to remember the last time he'd seen his mother smile and realized she hadn't done so since before Anna had left. He glanced at Tobias, saw he was too enthralled with his marble game to notice his absence, and went to where his mother stood. Ezra thought to tell her she needn't worry, that he'd spoken with his father, telling him not to come home. He refrained. As much as he wished it to be true, he knew his words had meant nothing to the man. Instead, he said the only truth he knew. "I hate Papa."

The startled look on his mother's face made him instantly regret his words. She glanced at the clock on the wall before lowering into a chair and motioning him closer. She placed her palm against his face. "You mustn't say things like that, Ezra."

"It's true. I hate Papa and wish he'd never come home!"

"Your papa loves you. He's loved you from the moment I told him you were to be."

"He's mean!" Ezra retorted. He could feel the tears welling in his eyes and struggled to contain them. "He makes you cry."

"It has not always been that way. Ever since he lost his job at the docks…your papa is a proud man." His mother's eyes grew moist. "Everything will be all right when he finds another job. You'll see."

Ezra could tell she didn't believe the words. He moved forward and sighed his relief as she gathered him into her arms, holding him while they both wept. After several moments, his mother released her hold on him, then used her apron to dry his tears. As Ezra watched his mother use the same stained apron to dry her own tears, he wondered why he'd never realized how useful the simple covering to be. He made up his mind right then and there that someday he would have a fine job and be able to buy his mother a new apron. Maybe blue, the color of the morning sky. That way, when he saw her with it on, it would remind him of the hope of the dawning day.

She turned, saw him smiling, and her lips curved ever so slightly. The rattle of the doorknob drew their attention and the moment was gone.

Chapter Two

The moment their father entered, Tobias gathered his marbles, retreating under a nearby table, and pulled his hat low as if doing so would render him invisible. For a moment, Ezra wished life offered him such luxuries. Instead, he turned toward his father, a fake smile plastered on his face. "Hello, Papa."

His father opened his mouth as if to answer, then shut it once more. Hanging his hat on the hook beside the door, he walked to the table and took his usual seat at the end, facing the kitchen area. Once seated, he placed a cloth bundle on the table. Ezra eyed the cloth but didn't chance to ask what it held, knowing the slightest misstep would uncap the rage within the man's calm exterior. As it was, his mother was already in danger of the man's wrath for not having dinner on the table when he entered the apartment. Ezra swallowed his guilt, knowing full well he was the reason for the delay. He wanted to say as much but kept silent, unwilling to incite the fury that was sure to follow.

His mother caught his attention and gave a subtle nod toward the dish cabinet. Ezra crossed the distance, holding his breath when he passed within his father's reach, only letting it out when he got to the cabinet without being struck. It didn't matter that he hadn't done anything wrong. In this house, breathing incorrectly was often enough to raise his papa's ire. He'd once been sent to bed without any supper over a simple sigh.

Opening the cabinet, he hesitated, knowing setting a place for his mother was unnecessary. She would place a spoonful or two on her plate and use her spoon to add it to his and Tobias' plate when Papa wasn't looking.

Deciding not to draw attention to the fact that there wasn't enough food, he counted four plates, placing them on the table without meeting his father's gaze. He returned to the kitchen, gathered the forks, knives, and spoons, then plucked the freshly washed linen napkins from the drawer. He placed a napkin next to each plate, carefully placing the silverware on top. Even with the meager offerings, his momma insisted on setting a proper table, saying doing so showed class. Not that there was anyone around to judge, nor did it matter that most of the silverware would go unused. His mother had told him she'd read it in one of her books, further telling him that someday when Papa found another job, there would be plenty of food, and they'd better know how to set a proper table.

He'd asked her if that also meant she wouldn't have to hide those same books from Papa. She'd simply sent him away with a look that made him sorry he'd asked.

Ezra returned to the cupboard, retrieved four glasses, and filled each with water from the faucet before placing one next to each dinner plate. As he sat a glass in front of his papa, the man lifted it to his lips with trembling hands. It was at that moment Ezra realized his papa did not reek of the stench that usually hung about the man like a cloak, stinging his nostrils when he ventured too close. Instantly, Ezra felt a glimmer of hope that maybe something he'd said in the wee hours of the morning had reached him.

His mother cleared her throat and Ezra realized he'd been staring at his father. Lowering his eyes, he slowly backed away.

His mother carried the beans to the table and scooped a serving onto Papa's plate. Her lips trembled as she placed a small spoonful onto her own plate before evenly dividing the rest between him and Tobias. She put the pan into the sink before repeating the process, placing a small spoonful of cubed potatoes on everyone's plate but her own. Lastly, she garnished Papa's and both boy's plate with a small johnnycake, cooked to a golden brown with crispy edges. Though there was no butter, Ezra's stomach rumbled its approval.

"Tobias, come eat your supper before it gets cold," she said firmly, then nodded for Ezra to take his seat beside his father.

His brother hurried into the room, both boys taking their seats just as their mother sank into her chair. It was the epitome of a happy family sitting at the table waiting to begin their evening meal, only no one at the table was smiling. Ezra and Tobias followed their mother's lead, placing the napkin on their laps.

Ezra dared a look at his papa. The skin around his mouth was white with beads of sweat forming just above his upper lip and at the edge of the man's temples. He'd seen that look before and it frightened him. Unless his words had indeed sunk in, it wouldn't be long before his father gave in to the drink that called to him.

Ezra remembered the bottle Papa kept in the cabinet above the glasses and wished he'd thought to hide it before Papa had returned. He swallowed, promising himself he would see to it tomorrow after Papa left for work.

His mother laced her hands together. Tobias copied her and Ezra did the same. She cleared her throat and Papa intertwined his fingers, resting them on the edge of the table to ease the trembling.

"Lord, thank you for this meal. Bless it so that it holds us until next we eat again. Amen," his mother whispered.

Ezra knew his mother's prayer was directed at his father. They were the words she used when there was no food available for the next meal. Said in the form of prayer, the words were less likely to provoke a fight. At least not at the table.

Papa raised an eyebrow and glanced at the meager offerings. He reached for the cloth sack he'd placed on the table, pushing it toward Momma, who sucked in her breath as she peeked inside.

"What is it, Momma?" Tobias asked, obviously

eager to see what had caused the reaction.

"Papa brought us some cheese." Momma didn't question where he'd gotten the cheese. She rarely criticized Papa, at least not in front of him or Tobias. They all knew he'd most likely won it gambling, another thing that was never discussed in the presence of the boys. She merely lifted the large hunk of yellow cheese from the bag, holding it up like a prize for all to see. Ezra knew it was her way of showing that while they might go to bed slightly hungry tonight, both he and Tobias would have something to fill their bellies in the morning.

Ezra's mouth watered. There hadn't been cheese in the house in months.

Tobias' eyes lit up. "Can we have some, Momma?"

"Tomorrow," Momma said, leaving no room for argument. She took the unused napkin from her lap and wrapped it around the cheese. She smiled at Papa. "We'll have it for breakfast in the morning."

Tobias sighed his disappointment and pulled his plate close, lifting his fork and dipping it into his beans.

Ezra was glad that Tobias knew better than to push the issue. Something like that was sure to set Papa off. Only after his brother began to eat did Ezra lift his own fork. There wasn't much on his plate, but the flavor was good. He looked at his mother's untouched plate and hoped that the knowledge of a morning meal would tempt her to eat her supper.

The sound of his father's fork scraping against his empty plate knew it wasn't to be.

His mother lifted her plate, offering her meal to Papa. To his credit, he hesitated before accepting.

Ezra wanted to scream at him, demand he give back the food. Couldn't he see Momma was ill? Fear of provoking the man's anger kept him silent. He lowered his eyes, unable to look in his mother's direction as he finished the food she'd given him. Tomorrow, he would refuse to eat unless she joined him. Tonight, his stomach was too empty to show such gallantry. Not for the first time, he felt anger toward the sister no one spoke of. At least when she lived in the house, there always seemed to be enough to eat. He knew the why of that. He'd gone with her enough to know she had a way of getting food even when no money lined her pockets. He thought of the day she'd shown him and Tobias how to lift apples from the applecart, and a plan started to form. He was tired of waiting for his papa to provide for the family, tired of going to bed hungry. If Papa wasn't going to be a man, then he would step up and see to it his mother and brother had enough to eat. Stealing food shouldn't be much more difficult than lifting an apple from the applecart. Ezra felt guilty knowing he would have to wait until tomorrow to put his plan in motion. Even as empty as his stomach felt, he'd still had a little something to ease the rumblings. His mother had seen to that.

The sound of his father's chair sliding away from the table caught his attention. His papa rose from the table, walking to the cabinet where he kept his bottle of spirits.

Ezra opened his mouth to beg him not to give in to

the temptation, but Momma placed her hand on his shoulder to silence him. He met her eyes and saw the fear that etched her face. The darkness wasn't gone. It had simply been delayed.

Chapter Three

Unable to sleep, Ezra lay in bed listening to his parents argue. Even though his bedroom door was closed, he could hear nearly every word. At first, it was only Papa's voice drifting through the walls in slurred accusations. Then, as if she could hold her tongue no longer, his mother's voice rose up, meeting his words with a sharpness of tongue that made him blush, saying things she'd never say if she'd known he was listening.

Ezra heard a sound and knew his father had silenced her the only way he knew. The way of a coward unable to withstand the biting words of truth. He wanted to fling open his bedroom door, walk the short distance to his parents' bedroom, and demand his father leave his mother alone. Instead, he buried his head beneath the pillow. Apparently, his father was not the only coward.

As he lay there, guilt clawing at his gut, he remembered the night before his sister left. A night very much like this where his parents' angry words drifted through the small apartment, sending icy chills down his spine. He remembered lying in the dark, wishing he could run away from the words and the monster that made him and the others live in constant fear. Instantly, everything made sense. Anna hadn't disappeared. She'd ran away. He wondered if it would be that easy to leave. *Anna never came back.*

He lowered the pillow from his head, a plan forming even as he did so. He was going to leave. He wondered for a moment if he should take Tobias with him but decided against it. Tobias would argue about leaving, and if he did, he might alert his papa. No, Tobias would have to stay here with Momma, at least until Ezra could find a job and come back for them. Could he get a job? *Anna had a job when she was not much older than me.* He had to; it was the only way. If his mother knew he had money enough to buy them food, she would come away with him. At least he hoped it to be true.

Ezra shook his pillow loose from the case and went to his dresser to gather his second set of clothes. He stooped in the dark to put on his shoes but decided to place them in the pillowcase instead. It wouldn't do for his papa to hear him leave. Ezra walked to his bedroom door and turned the knob, sucking in his breath as it clicked. As he exited the room, his stomach rumbled. It too seemed incredibly loud in the wee hours of the night when he was doing everything possible to remain quiet. He thought of the cheese Papa brought home and his mouth watered. He wondered if Momma would be angry if he carved off a thin slice to take with him.

Momma would wish me to have something in my stomach. Deciding it to be true, he tiptoed to the front door and placed the pillowcase on the floor. He'd nearly reached the kitchen when he realized the fighting had stopped. *If Papa comes out and catches me, it will not be good. Maybe they went to sleep.* He made his way to his parents' door, thinking to listen to see if they had indeed gone to sleep. As he approached, he saw a dim light trickling into the hallway and realized the door was ajar. He stood in the hallway for several moments before he gathered enough courage to push open the door just enough to see inside. The small lamp beside the bed proved just enough to see within the room. His breath caught as he saw his papa sitting on the far side of the bed, his back to him. He was just about to close the door when he saw his mother lying on the bedroom floor.

He wanted to run to her to make sure she was okay, but his feet wouldn't move forward. Tears streamed down his face as he ran from the room, his only thought to get away from Papa as quickly as possible. He unlocked the bolt and was halfway down the hall when he tripped, scraping the skin from his knees as he slid along the filthy floor. When at last he tumbled to a stop, he looked down the empty hallway, and a name bubbled to the surface of his brain.

Tobias! I can't leave him alone with Papa. There would be no coming back for his brother—he'd have to take him now. He pulled himself to his feet, mindless of his bleeding knees. Brushing away the tears, he forced his feet to move in the direction they did not wish to go. He paused at the door, opening it carefully to make sure his father was not in the room. He looked toward his parents' bedroom, pictured his mother lying on the floor, and instantly, his tears began to flow once again. He tiptoed to his brother's room, closing the door behind him. He walked toward the bed, reaching blindly in the dark until he found the string used to turn on the single overhead bulb. He closed his eyes, pulled the line, and then opened them once more. Tobias lay on the bed sleeping, oblivious to the ugliness that raged around him.

Ezra hurried to the bed and shook his brother. "Tobias, wake up."

"No, go away."

"Tobias, you need to wake up now," he whispered.

"Go away, or I'll yell for Papa."

Ezra fought the urge to leave Tobias where he lay and clasped his hand across his brother's mouth. He lowered his mouth to Tobias' ear and spoke as calmly as he could muster. "Papa has killed Momma."

Instantly wide awake, Tobias jumped from the bed blinking his disbelief.

Ezra pulled the pillow from its case and hurried to the dresser, opening drawers and shoving things inside the cloth sack. He handed Tobias the bag and motioned for him to follow as they soundlessly made their way to the door. Opening it as quietly as possible, he pushed Tobias into the hallway.

"Wait here. I'll be right back."

"Don't leave me out here!" Tobias yelled as Ezra started to close the door once more.

"Keep your voice down before Papa hears you. I'm

going to get some cheese for our breakfast."

"I want to come with you," Tobias insisted.

"No, it is safer out here. I'll leave the door open so you can see."

Tobias nodded, and Ezra breathed a sigh of relief. Grateful for the dim light that poured in from the hallway, he crept into the kitchen and found the linen napkin in which Momma had wrapped the cheese. Just thinking of his mother brought another onslaught of tears. Pushing aside his sorrow, he took the cheese to the counter and pulled a small knife from the drawer, using it to hack off a portion. Just as he'd finished separating it from the block, he smelled the stench of liquor. *Papa!* He turned, hoping he was mistaken.

"You little thief! How dare you steal from this family! Why, you're no better than one of those beggar boys on the streets."

Before he could move, Papa grabbed his arm. "Run, Tobias. Run and don't ever look back!"

The words had no sooner left his mouth when Papa's hand jutted forward, smashing into Ezra's face. Pain flashed. Papa inhaled a whoosh of air, and Ezra realized the knife was no longer in his hand. He wriggled from his father's grasp and stood there staring as his papa's face went white.

His father looked down then stared at Ezra with a puzzled look upon his face.

Ezra didn't wait to see what happened next. He hurried to the counter, grabbed the hunk of cheese he'd sliced, and raced from the apartment. He didn't slow down as he ran the length of the hallway and took the stairs two at a time, hoping to catch up with his brother before he left the building. It wasn't to be. Ezra rushed from the building, praying Tobias had enough sense to wait for him there. As he threw open the door, a dark blanket of fog greeted him. Even if Tobias were standing in front of him, he wouldn't have been able to see the boy.

"Tobias?" he whispered into the darkness. He looked over his shoulder before calling out his brother's name once more. When that too went unanswered, he walked down the front steps breaching the damp mist, and found himself at odds of which direction to turn. Deciding Tobias would have gone toward the market, he headed in that direction.

He felt numb as he took the familiar route, one he'd walked with his mother countless times before. His heart ached at the thought of never seeing his mother again. Had his father really killed her? If not, why was she on the floor? He pushed the image from his mind. He thought of the moments before leaving the apartment and wondered at the fate of his papa. He remembered the knife and how easily it had slid into his papa's gut. It had not been intentional. *Was it? Hadn't he just told his mother that he hated the man?* He'd merely wanted him to leave, not see him dead. *What if he is dead?* If he'd killed his papa, didn't that mean he was no better than the monster he claimed to hate?

The fog parted, and he saw a man standing under a street lamp only a few feet away. The man turned in his direction, the light showcasing his uniform. *A policeman*! Ezra locked eyes with the man. Fresh tears bubbled to the surface as he thought to call to the man, wishing to tell him about his mother.

"You there, what are you doing out here?" The policeman took a step in his direction. "What happened to your face, and what's in that bag?"

So many questions. Until that moment, Ezra hadn't even realized he'd stopped to gather his pillowcase, nor had he realized he had blood dripping from his nose. *If I tell him what happened, he'll send me to prison.* Icy fear shot through him and he took a step backward. The policeman charged him. Ezra managed to duck out of the way just as the man attempted to grab hold of his arm.

"Come back here, boy!"

Ezra sprinted off toward the market, taking several steps before the fog enveloped him once more. He couldn't see, but that was okay. It meant the police officer couldn't see either. He kept running, not taking a chance of the fog lifting. He slowed as he reached the market, straining to hear over the pounding in his chest. He couldn't hear footsteps, but that didn't mean he was alone. The fog parted. Ezra spun around, searching the empty market for any sign of Tobias. He wanted to call out to see if his brother could hear. But if he found him and the policeman proved to be near, Tobias would be in danger of being caught. His brother was a crybaby. If he'd happened to see what Ezra had done to their father, he would most assuredly tell the policeman what he'd seen. Tears welled in Ezra's eyes once more. He couldn't return home, nor could he continue looking for his brother until he was sure the policeman was no longer following him. He saw a wagon lined with bales of hay, and gave a moment's thought to scampering underneath to wait out the fog. *It will be the first place the policeman looks.* As he veered away from the wagon, a strong foreboding crept through him. He was alone. He wasn't sure which hurt more, his nose or his knees. Worse still, even though he was trying to be brave, he was terribly frightened. In that instant, he knew he'd never see any of his family again.

Chapter Four

Ezra felt something nudge his stomach, and opened his eyes. He looked up and saw an elderly man peering at him. The man's hat sat low on his head, the sleeves of his jacket settled well above the man's wrist. The weather was mild; in fact, he had yet to put on the shoes he'd stuffed into his pillowcase before running away. Nor was it raining, leaving Ezra to wonder why the man bothered wearing a coat in the first place. Maybe because it matched the green in his beady eyes, which in turn matched the hat upon his head. If not for the lack of a red beard, Ezra would have thought the man to be a leprechaun.

The man lifted his foot and Ezra realized the something he'd felt was the man's shoe. Ezra was up in an instant, raising his hands against the slap he expected to follow. He took a step backward, felt the cool brick wall pressing against his back, and knew he was at the mercy of the man who blocked the way forward and stood so close, Ezra could smell the garlic on his breath.

"Not to worry, lad, I don't mean to harm ye." While the man's words were encouraging, his scowl warned otherwise. "I ain't seen you around here before. New are ye?"

"Yes, sir," Ezra said, keeping his arms up in case the man changed his mind about wailing on him.

The man whistled a low whistle. "You're new, alright. Still got some semblance of manners too. Put your hands down, lad. I ain't ye pa."

Ezra lowered his arms but kept an eye on the man all the same. There was something peculiar about the stranger. "You know my papa?"

The man shook his head. "No, but I had my own pa once upon a time. Got tired of him using me for a punching bag. Left when I was about your age, I did."

"You did?"

"I said I did, didn't I?" The man looked him over. "How long you been on the streets?"

"I left yesterday," Ezra replied.

The man leaned in a bit closer and lowered his voice. "Decided yet?"

Ezra furrowed his brow. "Decided what?"

"Whether you're going back home or not. I told ye, I've been in your shoes," he said, straightening once again.

Ezra looked down at his bare feet and wiggled his toes.

This drew a chuckle from the guy. "Not in your actual shoes, lad. I just mean I know what you're thinking. You're scared and hungry and wish you were at home in your own bed. I thought about going back home. Thought about it a lot, I did. Never went, though.

But you, there's still time for ye. Sure your pa will be mad you went and ran away. You'll probably get a good scolding and most likely feel the hide of his belt on your backside, but you'll have a roof overhead once more. How does that sound?"

Ezra cast a glance at the stoop where he'd just spent the night, waking at every little sound. Apart from the belt on his backside, going home sounded good. Only he knew there was no chance of returning home. Not after what he'd done to his papa. Not for the first time, he wondered if he'd killed the man. Even if he hadn't, it wouldn't be the same without his momma there. Just the thought of her lying on the floor made his stomach churn. He started to tell the man that he couldn't go home but didn't trust himself to speak without bursting into tears. Instead, he shook his head.

The man peered at him through squinted eyes. "Why, you're shaking in your shoes. Ye must have done something godawful."

A tear trickled from Ezra's eye and he brushed it away with the back of his knuckle and stared without speaking.

The guy sighed. "Don't want to talk about it, then?"

Ezra shook his head once more. He heard a whinny and looked past the man to see a black horse hooked up to a wagon loaded with baskets of fresh vegetables. The horse's tail was swishing from side to side as if beckoning the man to come.

"Hold on there, Granny. I'll be with ye in a

moment," the guy called over his shoulder. "Old Granny's been with me so long, the lass she thinks she's my boss. That's her way of telling me I have to get the vegetables to the market. You listen to me, boy. This city ain't no place for a boy to be on his own. Either go home or find yourself a policeman. Tell him ye want a home and he'll take you to one of them asylums. The city's full of them. It might not be the best home, but it'll keep you off the street. You heed me on this: stay away from the gangs. The city is full of them too. The important thing is to stay off the streets at night. Get caught on the streets at night, and the gangs will tear you to shreds just to watch you bleed."

The horse neighed once again and the man backed away. "Remember what I said, lad."

Ezra nodded and watched as the man turned and walked to the horse, whispering something in her ear before climbing into the wagon. He looked in Ezra's direction, then turned and said something he couldn't hear. The horse answered with a nicker before slowly moving on her way.

Ezra replayed the man's words. *I can't find a policeman. He'll ask me why I'm on the streets. Even if I tell a lie, he'll know. Momma always knew when I told a lie. She said she could see it on my face. What if the policeman can see my lies too? Am I to join a gang, then? What if they don't want me to join? What if they find me on the streets in the dark and...* An image of his brother kneeling on the floor playing with his marbles came to mind. *Tobias!* He'd sent him into the dark and had given up looking for him. *Have I killed him too?*

Ezra snatched up his pillowcase and took off at a dead run, heading back to the only place he could think of. The market was bustling with activity when he arrived. He wandered amongst the crowd, hoping that luck would be with him and he'd find Tobias waiting for him. *Then what?* He pushed the question from his mind—no need to worry about the particulars until he found his brother.

Hearing a boy's laughter, he turned, only to be disappointed when the laughter proved to be from a little boy nearly half his brother's age. The boy's face was bright with adoration, his chubby fingers waving with delight as his black-socked legs dangled over the shoulders of a man Ezra presumed to be the kid's father. An image of his own papa sprang to mind. For a moment, Ezra was reminded of a long-ago time when he too used to laugh when riding high upon his papa's shoulders. That was before Papa had found the bottle more comforting than spending time with his family. Ezra glared at the pair, then turned, walking in the opposite direction.

His stomach rumbled and he remembered the hunk of cheese he'd shoved into the pillowcase. Stopping near the base of a wagon, he sat on a bale of hay and pulled the cheese from the bag. He took a bite and closed his eyes, enjoying the tang of the cheddar. He took several more bites before he remembered he was supposed to share the cheese with his brother. He took one more bite before returning the rest to the pillowcase, knotting the sack to keep the contents safely inside.

Ezra pushed off the hay, intending to continue his search. He'd taken but a few steps when he saw a small mound of cloth on the ground beside the wagon. He wouldn't have paid it any mind, except he recognized the little yellow flowers embroidered around the edges. *Tobias' pillowcase!* He knew it to be true, as his own pillowcase had the same yellow flowers. He raced to the mound, gathering the case from the dust and smacking it on the edge of the wagon in an attempt to remove the grime. He traced a hand over the flowers sewn onto the cases by their mother, remembering the day she had gifted each boy with a fresh case to cover their flattened pillows. It was the only Christmas present they'd received. Not that they minded. They hadn't even known it was Christmas until she'd had them each bring out their pillows, pulled them from their tattered cases, then shoved them into the new white cases. He'd slept soundly that night. Maybe it was because his momma had looked so pleased with being able to give them something she'd made just for them.

He turned the case over and sucked in his breath. A footprint covered the width of the case, but that wasn't what caused the chills that raced along his spine. The case, which had been clean when Ezra shook the pillow free the evening prior, was now splattered with droplets of blood. What the man said was true. *The gangs found*

Tobias and tore him to shreds! As the thought came to him, he dropped it onto the street and slowly backed away. There would be no reason to continue looking for his brother. Tobias was dead and it was his fault. He may not have killed him, but he'd yelled for him to run and hadn't found him in time to save him. Ezra bumped into the wagon and picked up his own case from the hay, only then realizing it was the same wagon he'd considered hiding under when he made his way to the market area after bolting from the apartment. He wondered if he would have bothered to circle around the wagon last night if he would have seen Tobias lying in the dirt. Or, maybe he'd have still been alive at that point, crouching on the other side waiting for Ezra to come save him. Instead, Ezra had been afraid of what Tobias would tell the police and that fear had cost his brother his life. Inching further from the wagon, Ezra turned, running blindly through the crowd, trying to escape the guilt that clawed at his heart.

Chapter Five

May 15, 1915

Ezra stood at the entrance of the bakery staring at the pastries that lined the shelves. Though he couldn't smell them, he longed to race into the store and plead with the store owner to part with a morsel or two. He wondered if she'd recognize him from the few occasions he'd visited the store with his mother and brother. It had been over a year since they'd had the money to go inside, but she'd spoken with his mother and had smiled at both him and Tobias, so maybe she would remember him and give him something to soothe his empty stomach.

The woman behind the counter looked up, saw him, and started in his direction.

She recognizes me. Ezra tried to smile, the effort pulling at his sore nose. He grimaced instead.

The woman reached for something as she neared the door. As she exited the store, she brandished a broom, jabbing it in his direction. "Away with you, urchin! You're so covered in filth, you're drawing flies. It's no wonder I haven't had a customer in the last few moments; you're scaring them all away! Be off with you. Don't come back, or I'll call the law on you and have 'em take you to the beggar's prison!"

Ezra opened his mouth to implore her to take pity on him, but before he could beg for her mercy, she smacked him on the head with the broom. Knowing he'd never get in her good graces, he turned, running as fast as his legs would carry him. When at last he slowed, he realized that in his panic, he'd run to the only safe place he knew, but a block away from the building he'd once called home. He ducked into the bushes in front of a nearby building and looked down the street with such longing that he nearly gave in to the desire to return home and take whatever punishment awaited him.

He can't punish me if he's dead.

The thought jarred him to his senses. Ezra looked at his pants, made a fruitless effort to brush away the blood and grime, and sighed. The only good part of his mother being dead was she was not alive to witness him walking about town looking like a beggar boy. It was no wonder the baker lady chased him. His own mother would have taken hold of both his and Tobias' hand if she'd passed the likes of him on the street. Ezra knew it to be true, as she'd done so on countless occasions, as if doing so somehow protected them from whatever evils had taken hold of the child and caused him to fall into such peril.

He brushed away a tear with the back of his hand. His knees hurt and he could tell he had torn open the scabs, causing them to ooze once again. The rest of him had not fared well either. His clothes were filthy, shredded at the knees and stained with dry blood.

Ezra ran his tongue over his chapped lips and sighed. His nose throbbed and he knew it was swollen, as he had trouble breathing with his mouth closed.

I want to go home.

He clutched the pillowcase to his chest, uncaring that it was as dirty as the rest of him. Knowing his mother had sewn it with her own hands gave him comfort and helped to dry the tears that still managed to fight their way to the surface whenever he let his guard down. Times such as this, all he wanted to do was curl into a ball. He inhaled like he'd seen his mother do on many occasions when she knew it was close to time for Papa to return.

If Papa sees me on the streets looking like this, the beating will be much worse. If I am to go home, I will need to clean myself up first.

He used the edge of the pillowcase to wipe the moisture from his eyes, then peeked inside the case. The clothes looked to be clean enough. Cleaner than what he had on anyhow. Still, his mother always insisted he wash up before changing, which was why he hadn't bothered to change before now. Besides, what good would it be to change into clean clothes if he was going to continue to sleep in doorways?

I'm not going to be sleeping in doorways. I'm going home. I'll take my punishment and that will be it. But what kind of home will it be without Momma and Tobias? Ezra pushed the thought from his mind. *Maybe Papa will be nice now. I don't eat much. Maybe he won't have a reason to drink if I don't complain about being hungry.*

Making up his mind to go home, he decided he needed to get cleaned up first. He'd go to the public bath but needed to be careful not to be seen by his papa before doing so. He knew there to be a free public bathhouse nearby, as his mother had taken them there for rain showers on occasion. The problem was he'd never actually gone there on his own and he knew he'd only be able to find the building if he started from the steps of their tenement building. He'd have to be careful not to be seen by his father, providing the man was still alive. While there were probably other ways to get to the bathhouse without passing in front of their building, leaving from here was the only way he knew.

Ezra heard the jangle of horse reins and looked to see a horse and carriage heading in the direction of the bathhouse. He sprinted across the street just as the buggy passed, and keeping the cart between him and the buildings, ran alongside until he felt it safe to continue on his own. From there, he was able to find his way to the massive stone building and step into line with the others waiting their turn to enter.

The woman ahead of him had two small blonde-haired boys in tow. The older of the two looked to be around Tobias' age. For a moment, Ezra fought to keep tears from returning. The boy turned toward Ezra, his brown eyes growing wide. He tugged on his mother's skirt. The woman turned, her expression upon seeing him looking much the same as the child's. She took hold of the boy's hand and pulled him in front of her as if the length of her skirt would protect him from whatever danger she perceived.

Once again, Ezra knew his own mother would have done the same if it were she standing there.

Every now and then, the boy would chance a peek around his mother's skirt. On one such occasion, Ezra stuck out his tongue. Not to be outdone, the boy returned the gesture.

Ezra attempted a silly face, but his nose throbbed, and he decided the action was not worth the effort.

The boy peeked around his mother's skirts once again. His mouth flew open and he tugged at his mother's skirt while pointing in Ezra's direction.

The woman turned to see what had upset the child, then clicked her tongue as she pulled a white handkerchief from the pocket of her skirt.

"Put this against your nose," she said, handing Ezra the cloth.

Ezra dabbed it to his nose, then pulled it away, surprised to see fresh blood.

"Keep the cloth pressed against your nose until the bleeding stops," the woman said firmly.

Ezra expected her to ask how he'd gotten injured, but she never did. Nor did she ask him to return the handkerchief. Even the boy seemed to lose interest in him as they slowly inched their way up the stairs of the building.

When at last they reached the entrance, the man at

the door glanced at the woman standing in front of him. His eyes traced the two children she had in tow, then spied Ezra standing behind her. Hoping to avoid questions about his appearance, Ezra sidled up next to the woman. The man scowled then nodded for them to enter without comment. If the woman noticed him pretending to accompany her, she never made mention of it. She merely scooped up the smallest child and hurried inside.

Ezra followed, parting ways when he reached the area set aside for men. An attendant wearing a white shirt with sleeves rolled to his elbows handed him a towel and a bar of soap then pointed to one of the shower stalls.

"Hey, kid, come back here," the guy called before Ezra had a chance to step inside. To Ezra's disappointment, he let the man behind him go next, telling him to wash and be quick about it. The man pointed to the tall stool beside the cart that held the towels and soap bars. "Put your stuff on there."

Ezra placed the towel and bar of soap on the stool and looked at the guy.

"Your sack too. Don't you go fretting. You ain't got nothing in that bag I need," the man said when Ezra neglected to set his pillowcase on the stool.

Ezra placed his bag on the stool but kept an eye on his belongings.

"Come over here and let me take a look at that nose of yours. I'll see if I can't get it straightened out for ya."

Once again, Ezra hesitated.

"Better let him take a stab at it, kid. You grow up with a crooked schnoz like that and you'll never get a woman worth looking at," a man near him said. To the amusement of those around him, the man made a show of pointing to his own nose, which pointed to the right side of his face.

Ezra took a step closer. The attendant stooped to his level and placed his fingers on either side of his nose.

"I'm going to be quick, but I won't lie to ya. It's probably going to smart a bit. I'm going to count to three. One, two, three." As the word left the man's lips, he stepped on Ezra's foot, using his fingers to crack Ezra's nose at the same time.

Tears sprang to Ezra's eyes as he sucked in a deep breath.

The attendant took hold of Ezra's chin, tilting it from side to side. "Not bad. Not bad at all."

"Why'd you go and step on my foot for?" Ezra grumbled.

"To take your mind off the pain in your nose." He straightened, looking down at Ezra as he did. "Did it work?"

"Well, my nose don't hurt as bad as my toes," Ezra admitted.

"Good." The man sounded pleased with himself. "You blow all that blood out of there and you'll be able to breathe better too. Now get your stuff and get in that rain shower. Take your time, kid. The steam will be good for ya."

"Hey, how come the kid gets to take his time and we don't?" the man with the crooked nose objected.

"You come over here and let me punch you in the snout and you can take all the time you want," the attendant retorted.

The man must not have wanted a long shower after all, as he kept his place in line. Ezra claimed his belongings from the stool, waited for the next rain shower to open, then limped into the stall.

Chapter Six

Ezra placed his clean clothes on the stool in the corner and ran the soap bar over his tattered clothes multiple times before stripping them from his body. Though the soap was no match for the dried blood, he was able to wash the grime from his pillowcase before rinsing everything under the falling water. Only after scrubbing his belongings did he bother to clean himself, staying under the rain shower until his fingers wrinkled. He turned off the shower, wrung the water from the items he'd washed, then placed them into the wet pillowcase before drying himself and dressing in the clothes he'd brought with him the night he'd left home.

He wasn't sure why the man had let him take his time but knew the same kindness would not be extended on his next visit. While he wished he had money to tip the man, the only thing he could offer was a grateful smile. The man nodded then went back to work, handing out towels and soap bars and yelling at the others to be quick about their business.

Ezra couldn't believe how much better he felt. With the dirt scrubbed from his knees and the ability to breathe from his nose for the first time in days, he practically strutted through the crowded hallway. Before leaving the building, he stopped, sitting on a bench in the hallway long enough to dry his feet and pull on his socks and shoes. If he were going to return home, he would make sure to return looking as respectable as possible. The last thing he wanted was to give his papa a reason to cuff him the second he saw him.

A small voice in the back of his head reminded him his papa was dead. He pushed that voice aside and started in the direction of the apartment. The closer he got to the building he'd called home since birth, the slower his pace became. His feet dragged as if they wished to go in the opposite direction. Even with his feet working against him, it didn't take long to walk the short distance. By the time he arrived, the small voice had returned and he was struggling to gather the courage to climb the steps to the apartment building. He gazed up at the window, half expecting his momma to be staring out at him. While the window was open, no one stood in front of it.

He paced back and forth in front of the brick building reliving the events of the evening he'd left. The fight between his parents, rousting his brother from his bed, then pushing him into the hallway. Telling Tobias to run, not knowing at the time he was never to see his brother again. He thought of the bloody pillowcase he'd found on the street at the marketplace, and pushed that memory aside. He couldn't deal with that today.

He remembered taking the cheese and staring into his papa's face. The memory was so fresh, he could almost smell the liquor that oozed from the man's pores.

If only Papa hadn't been drinking, then I wouldn't have had to kill him. Anger rushed through him and he threw the wet pillowcase he was holding at the building. *He's not dead. He can't be. If he's dead, I have no place to go.*

Tears fell from his eyes, and he brushed them away with the back of his hands. Ezra looked toward the window once more. *The only way to know for sure is to go inside.*

He retrieved his belongings, gathering the nerve to face the consequences of his actions. His legs trembling so badly, he could barely climb the stairs that he'd easily run up in the past, always preferring that than to smell the foul odors that came from so many living within the tenement building. But today, his legs chose to take their time and he had no recourse but to bide his time until he could see what fate awaited him. Upon arriving at the door to his apartment, the only thing that kept him from losing the contents of his stomach was that there wasn't anything to lose. He hadn't eaten anything for days.

He stood staring at the door, as if waiting for his mother to sense him there and come in search of him. He remembered all the times he'd entered and found her standing at the stove. She'd turn and offer him a brief smile to welcome him back home. He grasped the doorknob but still couldn't bear to open the door to the unknown. He stood there until the doorknob grew warm beneath his fingers before finally turning the knob and stepping inside.

The smell of fresh-baked bread greeted his nostrils the second he entered. He jerked his head toward the kitchen, surprised to see a slender woman standing at the stove with her back to him. Her hair was pinned. She had the lid to the pot in her left hand, her right hand busy stirring whatever was in the pot. A small boy sat on the floor near her feet. For the fewest of seconds, all the horror of the last five days melted away. "Momma!"

The woman turned. He saw the wrinkles that creased her thin face and knew in an instant it was not his mother. As if he were seeing the space for the first time, his eyes drifted around the apartment and he realized the living area was full of people. Strangers, more than he could count with both hands, sitting on the chairs, lying across the sofa, and others lying on makeshift pallets on the floor. Each had stopped what they were doing, looking at him as if it were he who was trespassing. If not for the fact that he recognized some of his family's belongings, he would have thought he'd entered the wrong apartment.

He took a step forward and the woman at the stove waved the spoon she'd been using in his direction, yelling words that made no sense.

He stopped but made no effort to leave.

The woman yelled once more then wiped her hands on the apron she was wearing—his mother's apron.

"Take off my mother's apron!" he yelled. He stepped toward the woman, intending to lay claim to the apron, when a man with a balding scalp and long grey beard stepped forward, blocking his way.

He took hold of Ezra's arm. "I don't know what's got you so riled, but you'll be leaving now before I see fit to toss you out that far window."

Ezra attempted to shake the hand free, but the man's grip held firm. He narrowed his eyes at the man. "What are you doing in my parents' apartment?"

The man nodded his understanding and relaxed his grip. "We live here. Four days since."

Four days? Ezra had slept on the streets five nights. That meant the family…no, families—there were too many to be just one—moved in the day after he left. He looked over the occupants, already knowing his parents weren't among them. If his momma were there, she would have already called to him. And his papa, well, he knew the man to be too proud to allow strangers to move into his home. Much to the landlord's chagrin, his family had been one of the few to live alone in the building. His mother had begged his father time and again to allow her to rent out one of the bedrooms to help pay the rent, only to have him tell her no.

When at last Ezra found his voice, his words came out on a croak. "My momma and papa?"

The man shook his head. "I do not know. I came in search of a place for my family and the landlord said I was welcome to move in here. There was another family traveling with me and the landlord agreed as long as they too paid rent. That is all I can tell you."

The woman at the stove bent and pulled two loaves of bread from the oven. Ezra's mouth watered. It had been a long time since there had been ingredients in the house with which his mother could make fresh bread.

Ezra pressed his fingernails into his palm to keep from crying. "She's wearing my mother's apron."

The man frowned, then said something to the woman in a language Ezra didn't recognize. The woman sighed and began untying the well-used apron.

Ezra pictured his mother lying on the floor and closed his eyes against the image.

Momma would wish her to keep it. "Tell her to leave it on. My mother no longer has any use for it."

The man repeated Ezra's words to the woman and she smiled a grateful smile. He looked around the room, his eyes settling on the door to the bedroom he once called his, wondering if the curtains his mother made were still hanging over the window. He swallowed, knowing the room to be exactly as he'd left it. Unable to handle any more disappointment, he turned to leave, the weight of the world heavy on his shoulders as he went. Just as he reached for the doorknob, a hand took hold of his shoulder. He was surprised to see the woman in the apron standing at his side. She presented him with a thick slice of the freshly baked bread, the center of which held a small pat of butter melting against the bread's heat. She laid a hand against his cheek, her eyes misting as she said words he didn't understand.

He looked to the man for translation.

"My mother's giving you the bread in exchange for the apron."

There were so many eyes upon him watching to see his response. Ezra knew the bread was intended for them. The stained apron was no great prize. Ezra wanted to refuse the offering, knowing his mother wouldn't approve. His stomach did not share his sentiment, as it growled a warning reminding him of his own hunger. As he took the bread, a tear slid from his eye. The woman lifted the apron and wiped it from his cheek the way his mother had done so many times. Unable to meet the gaze of those around him, he left. Pulling the door shut behind him, he slid down the wall fighting the emotions that gripped him as he bit into the warm bread. If his parents were not dead, they would still be in the apartment. He did not know what was to become of him, but at least for tonight, he had something to lessen the pain in his stomach.

Chapter Seven

Unwilling to venture out of his comfort zone, Ezra wandered around the market as he'd done most days since leaving his home. He also enjoyed the flurry of activity, as it helped ease his anxiety of facing the city on his own. The market was the last place he'd seen his sister, and a part of him hoped that she would suddenly reappear, promising himself that if she did, he would not be mad at her for leaving in the first place. If only she would return so that he wouldn't have to be alone. The market was where his brother met his demise, but he chose not to think of that, preferring to stay clear of that area altogether.

His stomach rumbled, but that was nothing new. Except for the cheese and bread, he'd not eaten anything since leaving home. He'd seen other children stealing from some of the venders, but each time he thought to do so, he'd remember what happened when he'd attempted to steal the cheese.

A woman strolled past with a basket piled high with tomatoes. His stomach rumbled once more and he pivoted, following at a distance. *I could do it. She wouldn't miss just one.* He thought of the cheese and his papa, but hunger kept him moving forward.

Just as he started to make his move, a dirty-faced boy badly in need of a haircut cut through the crowd and passed close enough to lift two tomatoes from the basket without the woman noticing. He slid one into his pocket and rubbed the other on the front of his filthy shirt before taking a bite. Ezra's mouth watered as juice from the tomato ran down the boy's chin.

His yearning turned to anger as the boy looked directly at him and took another bite. The boy smiled and Ezra narrowed his eyes. Undeterred, the boy took another bite. Ezra stepped forward, aiming to push the boy down and relieve him of his prize, when a police officer elbowed his way through the crowd and grabbed the boy by the scruff of the neck. The kid's eyes went wide. He looked over his shoulder, saw his captor, and squirmed to get away.

The officer firmed his grip on the boy. "Settle down, lad. You'll not be getting away this time. I hope you enjoyed that tomato. It'll be the last fresh thing you'll have for quite some time. It'll be off to the prison with you."

The color drained from the kid's face. Ezra watched the tomato fall to the ground, rolling a few feet before coming to a rest a few feet away. The police officer studied Ezra for a long moment before dragging the boy off in the opposite direction.

Ezra wasted no time retrieving the half-eaten tomato. He wiped the dirt away best he could before shoving the whole thing in his mouth, closing his eyes and enjoying the acid goodness of the sun-warmed fruit. The precious morsel did little to relieve his hunger. He thought of the woman with the basket and wondered where she'd retreated to. As if someone had knocked him alongside his head, he realized how close he came to getting caught. The boy was obviously more experienced and had lifted the fruit without the woman's knowledge. If the police officer had not seen him, he would have gotten away with his crime. Ezra knew, with his lack of experience, he would have been caught much sooner and it would have been he who'd been carted off to prison. A chill rolled the length of his body. He remembered the day his sister left and how she'd showed both him and Tobias how to pick apples. While he'd managed to pluck an apple from the cart that day, he'd not been as successful when he'd next attempted it. He'd been in this very market when he'd gotten caught. If not for his mother giving the man part of the money Papa had given her to buy food, he too would have gone to prison that day. As it was, his momma had made him promise he would never steal again. A promise he'd forgotten the night he made his decision to leave, and look at everything that had happened since then.

Ezra sighed and looked to the sky. *I'm sorry, Momma.*

I'll starve before I try to steal again. Not knowing what else to do, Ezra wandered aimlessly around the market. For some reason, his drifting took him to where he'd found Tobias' pillowcase, a place he seldom went. He kept his eyes averted until after fully passing the wagon. He'd not gotten very far, when he saw the old man who'd spoken to him on the steps the morning after he left home. He knew it to be the same man, as he was wearing the same green jacket and hat as before. The man was busy loading vegetables into the basket of a woman standing in front of him. Ezra passed unnoticed then circled around to the far side of the wagon. Though it was later in the afternoon, there were still plenty of vegetables on the wagon, most within reach if anyone dared give it a try. Still traumatized by the earlier event, and adamant about keeping his new promise, Ezra kept his hand pressed securely in his pocket as he strolled past. Clearing the wagon, he crossed the sidewalk and leaned against the building, watching the man sell his fruits and vegetables. Every now and then, the crowd would thin and the man would turn and look in his direction. If he recognized Ezra, he made no move to call to him, nor did Ezra go out of his way to let his presence be known. Though he didn't have any ties to the man, something about his presence eased his anxiety and he remained there the rest of the day watching the man sell his wares. As the market crowd dwindled, the man made preparations to leave. He untethered Granny from the post, clicking his tongue so that the horse moved backwards from the curb. Once free from the space, he moved the bales of hay in front of the opening that defined his space in the market. He walked to the wagon, then returned a moment later, laying a small parcel on the hay. Only after he'd settled onto his cart did he look in Ezra's direction and give the faintest of nods toward the parcel before shaking the reins and calling to Granny to take them home.

Ezra waited for him to leave before hurrying to see what it was he'd left. To his surprise, he found two large carrots, a few green beans, and an overly ripe tomato. Though they were raw and somewhat bruised, it was food. Ezra scooped up the offerings and rushed back to where he'd bided his time that day. Crouched with his back planted firmly against the brick building, his eyes darted from side to side as he choked down the food. While it wasn't much, he was going to make sure no one got near enough to take his supper.

***

Friday, May 21, 1915

Ezra sat on the hay bale watching for the man in green to return. He saw him coming, then hurried to push the hay out of the way. This was something he'd done since the day the man had left the food. Once Ezra cleared the opening, he hurried to his place near the building without a word. The two had reached a silent agreement—Ezra moved the hay each day, and in return, the man left him a small token of raw vegetables. Not the most satisfying diet, but it kept him from starving to death.

Granny turned into the opening without any

49

prompting from the man, who then climbed down from the cart and looped the horse's tether to the post. He looked at the bucket of fresh water, then looked in Ezra's direction. Ezra smiled, and the man gave a slight nod before turning his attention to the wagon, getting things ready for the Friday crowd. Every day was a busy day in the market, but Fridays and Saturdays more so as those were the days when hourly workers collected their pay. They were also the days the street kids showed up in droves, knowing the increased hustle and bustle would give them added cover. His mother used to hate going to the market on those days, saying she must be extra diligent in watching her coin purse.

Ezra only knew it to be Friday, as he'd overheard one of the men telling the others to keep a watch out for the street Arabs today lest they steal them all blind. A few of the men had looked in Ezra's direction after hearing the remark, but no one had bothered to shoo him away.

The vegetable man stood at the back of the cart selling his wares, when Ezra noticed a boy several years older than himself inching his way toward the side of the wagon. The boy's hat was pulled low over his forehead, but from his vantage point, Ezra could see his eyes skimming the contents within the wagon and knew he was moments away from stealing from the man. Ezra thought to call out to the man, but he was in the middle of haggling with a fellow, and Ezra didn't want to disrupt the sale.

Ezra watched as the boy moved to the wagon,

dipped his arms over the side, and grabbed hold of a basket overflowing with dark green cucumbers. Granny nickered at the boy, but the man in green never turned to see what had gotten her riled.

As the boy lifted the basket from the wagon, something inside Ezra snapped. He pushed from his spot, racing forward, his shoes flying from his feet as he ran. He tucked his head, ramming into the kid and knocking him to the ground with such force that the basket flew into the air, sending the cucumbers rolling in all directions. The boy recovered quickly and began pummeling Ezra with his fists. A whistle sounded, and Ezra felt himself pulled into the air, his heart sinking as he saw it was a policeman who'd pulled him free. *I'm going to prison.*

Another policeman had a grip on the thief, who was glaring at Ezra for all he was worth. The boy spit at Ezra and the policeman smacked the kid alongside his head.

"Two more rats off the street," the policeman said, leading him away.

"Wait!"

Both Ezra and the policeman who held him turned to see who had spoken. Ezra felt a glimmer of hope when the vegetable man stepped forward, removing his hat.

He gave a nod in Ezra's direction. "That lad's with me. He helps with the horse while I tend to the vegetables and I pay him in kind."

"You're telling me he wasn't trying to steal from you?" The policeman didn't sound convinced.

"Not at all. If he'd wanted to do so, he's had many opportunities. No, sir, that boy is an honest one. He was merely trying to prevent that one from relieving me of that basket of vegetables." He frowned at the overturned basket, peered at the other kid, and sighed. "Why, the dirty bugger has cost me dearly. I'll never get a reasonable price for them now that he's bruised them."

"It's not the boy's fault," Ezra interjected. "He wouldn't have dropped them if I hadn't butted into him with my head."

The vegetable man gaped at Ezra for several seconds as if trying to figure out what to say next. Finally, he smiled and returned his hat to his head. "What did I tell you? The boy is honest as the day is long."

The policeman must have agreed with him, as he turned him loose. Once freed, Ezra dropped to the ground gathering the cucumbers and placing them into the basket. When he'd finished, he put the basket back in the wagon and returned to his spot near the building.

The remainder of the day passed without excitement. People came and went, and the vegetable man sold his produce, including the cucumbers, which hadn't looked at all bruised. When at last he'd sold everything and backed the wagon from its place, Ezra ran to move the hay in front of the opening. As expected, the man had left him something in return. As he picked up the little bundle, he hesitated. It felt different. Tears sprang to his eyes as he peered inside and saw a fresh meat pie. He pulled the treasure to his chest and turned to the man.

"Thank you, sir."

The vegetable man tipped his hat, clicked his tongue, and Granny moved forward.

Ezra sat on the hay bale, tears stinging his eyes as he bit into the meat pie. While he'd taken to sleeping within the confines of the hay, it was the first night he felt it okay to have his evening meal in the area he now called home.

Chapter Eight

May 22, 1915

Ezra pulled the hay bales aside then started for his usual spot against the wall.

"Lad, if you're going to be working for me, you'd better stay close," the vegetable man said as Granny pulled the cart into their spot.

Ezra stared at the man in disbelief. "You mean a real, honest-to-goodness job?"

"Now don't go getting too excited. If ye do what I tell you and help keep the street rats from stealing me blind, I'll see to it ye have a coin or two in your pocket at the end of each day."

Ezra sighed his disappointment. He'd hoped the man would be willing to pay him with another meat pie.

Granny stopped, and the vegetable man jumped from the wagon and tethered her to the post. Ezra wasn't sure why he bothered, as the horse never made any attempt to move except to use her tail to swat the flies away. Sometimes she drank from the bucket, but mostly she stood with her head hung low. The man walked to the back of the wagon, pulled the board free, and slid it in between the baskets. After he'd pulled several baskets forward, he turned his attention back to Ezra.

"I believe a few coins to be fair wages for a day's work. If you think you can do better, then you'd best be getting to it. From the looks of things, if you don't do something quick, you'll soon starve to death." The man looked him over. "You look to be in worse shape than Ol' Granny there, and she ain't nothing but bones these days."

"Why no, sir, I think that's quite fair. It's just as you say. I'm mighty hungry, and I thought maybe I'd rather be paid with a meat pie," Ezra explained.

The man took off his hat and scratched his head. "Lad, you could buy several meat pies with what I aim to pay ye."

While more meat pies sounded just fine, Ezra felt bad taking advantage of the man's generosity. "I think I can get by with only one, sir."

"You are the most peculiar lad I've ever met. Why, ye could have a meat pie and even have a few coins left to find yourself a safe place to sleep at night. You can't sleep next to that wall all night."

"Sir, I must confess. I've been sleeping right here at night." Ezra felt a blush creep up his face. "Right next to the hay. It's not so bad. The policemen walk the street a lot at night to keep the kids away from the wagons."

The man sighed. "I tell you what I'm going to do. I'll bring ye a meat pie each day and I'll keep a tally of the rest. If you ever decide to move on, I'll pay you what I owe. That settle right with you?"

"Yes, sir," Ezra said, bobbing his head.

"We better shake on it, then." He extended his hand to Ezra and the two shook on the deal. "The name's Angus."

Ezra wasn't sure if that was the man's first or last name, as the man never offered more. "I'm Ezra."

"Good to meet you, Ezra. Now tell me why is it ye never did what it was I told you to do?"

"What's that, sir?"

"That day on the stoop. I told ye to either go home or find yourself a police officer. Obviously, you ignored my good advice. You had plenty of opportunities to steal food from me, but ye didn't. Why would a boy like yourself prefer to starve on the streets than to heed sound advice? Why, if I hadn't left you food each night, you'd be dead long before now."

"Thank you for your kindness."

Angus laughed. "Boy, that wasn't kindness. I barely left ye enough to keep alive. I'd hoped you'd get tired of being hungry and follow my advice. But instead, ye hung around like a dog looking for scraps."

Ezra couldn't figure Angus out. While he smiled when he spoke, it sounded as if he didn't want him around. He turned to leave.

"Now where ye off too?"

"You just said you didn't want me hanging around begging like a dog."

"We're past all that now. I ain't feeding you scraps no more and you ain't begging. You'll be earning what I give ye. I just wanted to know why you didn't return home."

"I did," Ezra said without looking at Angus.

"Don't tell me your parents wouldn't let you stay."

"They weren't there."

"So they weren't at home. You could have waited for them or gone back later."

"No," Ezra said softly. "You don't understand. My family is dead. There were others living in the apartment. A woman had on my mother's apron."

Angus rocked back on his heels. "Just because they moved away without telling you don't mean they be dead."

Ezra looked Angus in the eye for the first time. "I killed them."

People were beginning to pour into the marketplace now. A woman stepped up to the cart. Angus looked Ezra in the eyes. "Don't ye go nowhere."

Not having anywhere to go, Ezra nodded his head. Angus helped the woman and countless others before he was able to continue their conversation. He lifted Ezra, sitting him on the back of the wagon with ease that belied his age. "You won't steal food, but you're going to sit there and tell me ye killed your parents?"

"Yes, sir. And my little brother Tobias too."

A woman approached the cart and Angus let out an exasperated sigh. "Don't move."

Ezra remained seated as Angus conducted the transaction then turned to him once again.

"Tell me what happened," he said firmly.

"I wanted to talk to Papa about his drinking. It's best to do that before he starts, so I was up when he came out of his bedroom." Ezra decided to leave out the part of his being too hungry to sleep. "I talked to him and asked him not to go, but Papa said it didn't matter, saying the drink would continue to call to him until he answered. So I told him not to come home. He did. Come home, that is, and I think that's why he killed Momma."

Angus interrupted. "I thought ye said you killed her."

"I did. Papa and Momma have had fights before, but he didn't kill her until I told him to stay away." He was crying now, but he didn't care. It felt good to be rid of the secrets he carried. When Angus didn't respond, he continued. "I fell asleep, and when I woke up, I heard Momma and Papa fighting. I made the decision to leave that very night, but I was going to go alone. I thought if I were to get a job that Momma would agree to come away with me. Her and Tobias— he was my little brother. Only, as I got ready to leave, I realized they'd stopped fighting. I went to their room. I don't know why, because if Papa had caught me, he would have been furious. I pushed open the door. That's when I saw Momma on the floor. Papa didn't see me, so I ran to wake Tobias and told him what Papa had done and to wait in the hall. Papa came out…"

Angus waited on five customers then nodded for him to continue.

Ezra thought about ending his story there. Angus

only asked him to come work for him because he thought him to be honest. He swallowed. Lowering his eyes, he continued. "Papa caught me stealing the cheese. I wasn't, though; I was only going to take enough for me and Tobias to share for breakfast. I didn't take Momma's portion, even though I knew she wouldn't be there to eat it. But Papa was real mad. He hit me in the face, and I… I had the knife in my hand and then it was gone. I could tell by Papa's face I'd hurt him real bad. I screamed for Tobias to run and he did. Then I ran too. Only I wasn't sure which way Tobias had run and there was this policeman and I thought he would take me to prison for what I'd done. I didn't mean to leave Tobias all alone, but I was afraid if the policeman found him, he would tell the man what I'd done. So I left, thinking to find him in the morning. That's when I first saw you and you told me what the gangs would do. I ran in search of him. But I was too late. The gangs got to him just as you said. They tore him into tiny pieces and not even his bones were left. Just some blood."

Ezra was sobbing uncontrollably now. A lady approached, saw him crying, then left without a word.

Angus made no attempt to call her back. Instead, he handed Ezra the handkerchief from his coat pocket. "If you didn't see your brother killed, how do you know it to be true?"

"I told you I saw his blood." Ezra sniffed.

"You said that, but how can you be certain it was his?"

"Because I found the pillowcase our mother made him. I'd shoved it into his hands before he left. I found it right over there," Ezra said, pointing his chin in the direction of the wagon where he'd found Tobias' pillowcase.

Angus looked toward where Ezra had gestured. A moment passed before a slow smile spread across the man's face.

Ezra was incensed. "It's not funny!"

"No, if it were as ye said, it would not be," Angus agreed.

"It happened. I saw the blood," Ezra insisted.

"The blood you saw did not belong to your brother."

"It was his pillowcase."

Angus raised a hand to silence him. "I'm telling ye I saw what happened that day. It was right after I left you. I arrived to find your brother and several other lads having it out with the man who owns that wagon. I'd seen the other boys around—they used to sleep under that wagon at night. It was the first time I saw your brother, a small lad to be sure—full of piss and vinegar that one. Why, the man that owns the wagon had no sooner grabbed hold of the lad than your brother bit the fellow's leg. That's where the blood came from. Your brother got away clean. He was the talk of the market for days. Tore a chunk right out of that leg, he did. Sent the man to the hospital."

Ezra blinked his surprise. "You mean my brother's still alive?"

Angus shrugged. "I can't say, but he was when he left here. That I can attest to."

Ezra jumped from the wagon.

"Hold on there, boy, where are you going?"

"Why, to find my brother, of course."

"And just where do ye plan on looking? There are millions of people living in the city and more pouring in from Ellis Island every day. I'll not be stopping ye from leaving, but I think you'd have a better chance if you stay here. If your brother wants to find ye, this is the first place he'll look."

Ezra looked around the marketplace. Angus was right. Even if his brother were here, there were so many people wandering about that Ezra wouldn't be able to find him. While he wished he could find Tobias, he knew what the man said to be true. In a matter of seconds, he'd gone from sorrow at being responsible for his brother's demise to envying the boy. For at the moment, he knew his brother to possess something he did not. The courage to make it on his own.

Chapter Nine

June, 1915

Ezra stood on a hay bale, keeping a close eye on the crowd around the wagon. Women and men all clamoring to be next. It had been this way since Angus arrived, though Ezra wasn't sure why.

"Lad, climb up there and push forward another basket of grapes," Angus called over his shoulder.

Ezra jumped from the hay bale and used the wheel to climb into the wagon. He looked over the produce—tomatoes, carrots, onions, and several baskets of various beans—before admitting defeat. "Which are the grapes?"

Angus held up a cluster of deep purple balls. Ezra moved aside a basket of green beans and pushed a basket loaded with the balls closer to Angus, causing a renewed surge of excitement to race through the crowd. Ezra shook his head, wondering why people were so excited about what looked to be a bunch of marbles. An image of Tobias sitting on the floor playing with his marbles came to mind. Ezra cupped his hand over his eyes and surveyed the crowd, wondering if his brother was amongst them. It wasn't the first time he'd done so, but as always, his brother was nowhere to be seen. Sighing, he sat on the side of the wagon waiting to be of assistance.

As the day lingered, the weather warmed, sending a sheen of sweat glistening across Granny's back. Ezra jumped from the wagon, tested the temperature of the water in her bucket, then dumped it on the ground. He took the pail to the spigot a few buildings down, filled it, then lowered his mouth to take a drink. By the time he'd given Granny fresh water and returned to the wagon, his skin was as shiny as the horse's back. He climbed back onto the wagon, looked at Angus, and frowned. How the man could wear that jacket on such a hot day baffled him.

With the size of the crowd, they sold out earlier than usual. The only thing that remained was a basket full of produce, which Angus kept to take home at the end of each day.

Angus climbed up into the wagon, removed some straw from one of the baskets, and pulled out a large cluster of grapes. He sat on the back of the wagon and motioned for him to join him. "Take the weight off your legs."

Ezra happily obliged and Angus handed him one of the balls, copying Angus as he popped one into his mouth. As he chomped down, the ball exploded in his mouth, a burst of tangy sweetness that made him giggle. He crunched through a couple of seeds and swallowed. He then slid a glance to the remaining cluster. Angus chuckled and pulled one of the stems free. He handed it to Ezra, who wasted no time plopping another into his mouth, once again delighting in the explosion of tangy-sweet flavor.

Angus laughed. "I take it you've not had grapes before."

"No, sir."

"Now you see why we had such a crowd today," he said, handing him another stem.

"I do," Ezra said, frowning at the purple stain on his fingers.

"It'll come off. But I don't think that's what has your face in a knot. What's on ye mind, lad?"

"I don't understand why you grow vegetables with so little taste when you can grow these."

Angus gave a nod to the cluster. "Grapes are a fruit. Still, every vegetable has its purpose. And though I know it's hard to believe, there are people who do not like grapes. Especially when they're picked before they turn sweet."

Ezra felt his eyes grow wide. "What kind of person does not like grapes?"

"I don't grow them," Angus said, ignoring his comment. "I don't grow any of them."

Another surprise. "You don't?"

"No, I go down to the railroad or docks each morning and collect my wares from the trains and ships that come in. I said something to trouble you," Angus said when Ezra's mood soured.

"My papa used to work on the docks. He was happy

then."

"What happened to change that?"

"My momma said he lost his job. I asked her if I could help him find it, but she said it wasn't like that."

"No, I suppose it was not," Angus said, pushing the sweat from his forehead with the sleeve of his jacket.

"Why do you wear that?"

"What?"

"The jacket. It's so hot out, I can hardly breathe, and I don't have shoes on." He wanted to add that the jacket made Angus look like a leprechaun but thought better of it.

"You don't have shoes on because you don't eat enough to keep them from falling off your feet," Angus reminded him.

Ezra ignored the comment. "Are you not hot?"

"I get hot, sometimes. But not as much as you'd think. The coat is made to breathe."

Ezra peered at the coat. "Are you saying it's alive, then?"

This elicited another chuckle. "No, not in the way you're thinking. But it does bring me comfort."

Ezra thought of the pillowcase he kept near him when he slept and nodded.

"You understand, then?"

Ezra nodded once more.

"It also makes sure I have a bit of money to line my pockets."

"So you are a leprechaun, then," Ezra blurted, then

covered his mouth.

"I'm Irish to be sure, but I'll no be a leprechaun." Angus elbowed Ezra. "Go get the meat pies from the basket and I'll join ye for supper while we talk."

Ezra hurried to do as told, eager to have someone to talk to for a change. He handed one to Angus and unwrapped the other, taking a bite as he sat.

"How old are ye, lad?"

"Seven."

"I thought ye to be round the age I was when I left home."

"You said you had a papa like mine. Is that why you left home, 'cause he hit you?"

"Aye, among other things."

"Did your papa drink?"

"No, I was born in '42, 1842 that is, right before the start of the Great Hunger." He sighed. "Some call it An Gorta Mor—the Potato Famine, but I lived it and I think the Great Hunger fits it better."

Ezra wasn't sure what a potato famine was, but he knew what it meant to be hungry.

"I ran away when I was a wee lad of eight, so that'd be 1850. I was pretty lucky, as I found me a fellow that had a bit of money. He was a landlord and I was not supposed to have any dealings with them, as they treated people bad and tried to starve us off our land. My da would have been a might sore if he knew me to be there. The man, the landlord, he let me sleep in the barn and his wife fed me a bit, she did. Not a lot, mind ye, but I ate enough to get by. Then one day, that fellow's wife died and the landlord made the decision to come to America. Told me he'd bring me with him and I could continue to work for him. What he didn't tell me is that I were to be his indentured servant. You know what that is, lad?"

Ezra shook his head.

"I didn't either, not at the time. Truth be told, I would have gone even if he'd told me and explained what it meant. I was fifteen years old and had nothing better to do. He had me make my mark on a paper saying he would pay for my transportation to America, and in exchange, I had to work for him for five years."

Ezra smiled. "So he gave you a job."

"You could call it that, only I didn't get paid. And I couldn't quit because I'd made my mark. Mr. Twomey—that was the man's name—paid my passage alright. Steerage. You think it smells around here; you take all the people you saw in the market today, then add some more and put them all in the belly of a ship. That's how it were. We'd take turns standing and sleeping. Still, I was lucky."

Ezra blinked. "You were?"

"Aye, I was working for Mr. Twomey, so I got to go topside and shine his shoes, fetch him his paper, and whatever else he wanted me to do."

Ezra wasn't sure why Angus sounded so riled; he wouldn't mind doing those things if Angus asked. He got his answer when next the man spoke.

"Something happened after the missus died. Mr.

Twomey had always been short-tempered, but it got worse. Then, during the trip over, he fell into the drink. I guess being on a ship that long causes a man to get bored. But just like ye papa, when Mr. Twomey fell into the drink, he turned mean as a jackal. I won't go into details, but I wasn't liking working for him. It got worse when the ship arrived here in America."

Ezra's papa was always complaining about people coming in off the ships. "That's when you came to Ellis Island, right?"

"No, lad, me and Mr. Twomey came over in 1857, so we came in through Castle Gardens. Ellis Island didn't come about until some years after that."

Ezra sighed, but Angus didn't seem to notice.

"One day, we were out about town, and I was carrying groceries for Mr. Twomey, and well, he'd bought a lot, so I was struggling to carry it all. I tripped. Mr. Twomey was full of the drink and started beating me the way one would a dog they wanted to run away."

"You ran away?" Ezra asked.

"No, I couldn't, as how I'd made my mark. If I ran away, the police would have made me go back. But what happened was that this man happened to be riding by in his wagon and made Mr. Twomey stop. Mr. Twomey didn't want to. He said I was his property for another three years until my contract was up."

Now Ezra was intrigued. "What happened?"

"The man, Mr. Maguire, pulled out his wallet and offered to buy my contract."

"Did he agree?"

"He hemmed and hawed a bit, but in the end, he did."

"And you went to work for Mr. Maguire?"

"I did that very night."

"And you never saw Mr. Twomey again, did you?"

"Actually, I did."

Ezra sighed.

"Now it's not as bad as all that. You see, the next time I saw Mr. Twomey, he looked might well. He had a fine lady on his arm, and she a wee baby in hers. He told me he'd stopped with the drink. I didn't smell it on him, so I know it to be true."

Ezra thought of his own papa and sighed. "Did you like the other man?"

"Mr. Maguire? I liked him very much, but I liked his daughter even more. I married her in 1862, the same day my servitude was up. With her father's blessings, I might add."

"You mean to tell me you're married?" Ezra asked.

"Not anymore. But I had forty-eight years with me fair Darla. I lost her five years ago. The why of it isn't important; she got sick and died."

"Did it make you want to turn to the drink?"

"What?"

"Your wife dying. You said when Mr. Twomey's wife died, he turned to the drink."

Angus smiled. "No, lad, I'm stronger than the drink."

"I wish my papa would've been stronger than the drink," Ezra said softly.

After a few moments of silence, Angus pushed from the buckboard, removed the long plank, and slid it into the slot at the end of the cart. He tilted his head toward the sky and grimaced. "We'll be getting some rain tonight. I suspect Granny and I better be heading for home."

Ezra climbed over the side of the wagon and ran to untie the tether so that Angus wouldn't see his disappointment. He handed up the reins and stood on a bale of hay while Granny backed the wagon into the street. As soon as the wagon cleared, he lugged the hay bale in front of the opening.

Granny started forward and Ezra went to fetch the second hay bale. As he turned, he was surprised to see Angus and Granny paused just a few feet away.

"Come on then, lad. I'll no have you being washed away with the rats."

Chapter Ten

Ezra wasted no time climbing up into the wagon and taking a seat on the bench next to Angus, who clicked his tongue to get the horse moving. Though he'd been in the back of the cart numerous times, it was the first time he'd ridden in it. Granny slowly click-clopped her way down the street, pausing now and again when a person or motorcar blocked her way. Sitting there watching the buildings pass by, it didn't take long before Ezra saw sights he hadn't ever seen before, including buildings being erected before his very eyes. Ezra stared in awe, tipping his head back as far as it would go, watching men standing on beams so high in the sky, it looked as if they could touch the clouds. The men walked without care, crossing the narrow beams and carrying what looked to be buckets to the other side of the building.

"Ye keep your mouth open like that, and you're going to swallow a bug," Angus said with a laugh.

Ezra gaped at the men overhead. "Are they not afraid they will fall?"

"Aye, I suppose they've been doing it long enough they know where to place their feet, doncha know. Think ye'd like to work that high?"

No! "I wouldn't be scared," Ezra said, then instantly regretted lying to the man. "Well, perhaps I'd be a little scared."

"No shame in being afraid. I'd not likely climb out on that plank even if I was not such an old man. I'm happy to keep my feet planted firmly on the ground. That's what has kept me on this side of the dirt all these years. Why, one miss-step and there wouldn't be enough of a fellow to scrape off the dirt for a proper burial."

"Do you think anyone has ever fallen?"

"Aye, to be sure. Many men have given their lives to building this great city."

"I don't think I want a job where I might die," Ezra said softly.

"Hunger is a good sauce," Angus said softly. "A man never knows what he's capable of until he sees his children hungry."

"Not my papa. We were always hungry, but Papa didn't care. He'd rather drink than work."

"In Ireland, there is a saying. A man takes a drink, the drink takes the drink, the drink takes the man."

"What's that supposed to mean?" Ezra asked.

"Ye said yourself; it was better to speak to your da before the drink had hold of him. Once the spirit takes hold, it takes control—the drink takes the man. I bet your da wished he could control the drink. Why, I'd bet he no more wanted to take that drink than you wish to climb up that building and take a walk across that beam."

Ezra thought of his papa and momma and sighed.

Angus clamped a boney hand on Ezra's shoulder. "Do not let your heart be heavy, lad. Guilt will gnaw at a fellow until there is no more goodness left in his soul. Your parents can help ye no more, but you can help yourself. Put the darkness behind you and let the light shine on the lad you are to become."

Ezra wasn't sure how to put the darkness behind him. Nor how to let the light shine, but he was happy at having Angus sitting next to him. While he didn't understand all the man's words, it was nice having someone to talk to. He wanted to tell the man that but didn't know how to put his thoughts into words, so instead, he remained quiet as he watched the landscape change around them.

"Never been down this way, have ye?" Angus asked after a bit.

"No, sir. I've never ridden in anything that moved before either."

"Not even a trolley or bus?"

"No, sir."

"What if ye had to get somewhere?"

"The only place we ever went was to the market. Or maybe the rain shower. Both were close, so we walked."

"From the way you talk, I'd have thought your family to have had money," Angus replied.

Ezra shrugged his shoulders. "Everyone talks."

"Yes, but not everyone speaks well," Angus replied.

Ezra still wasn't sure what the man was getting at. "You speak okay."

"That's because you haven't heard me speak the

Gaelic." He smiled. "You will. It slips out on occasion. I speak well enough now. Though such was not always the case. When I first came over on the boat, my Irish was so thick, some couldn't understand me; why, even my dear sweet Darla had trouble understanding me at times. She worked with me to help me speak plain so we could converse properly. I think that pleased Mr. Maguire since he saw that Darla and I were getting along so well. He said a man could sound educated even if it wasn't true. Said it would help me get a good job."

"What kind of job did you get?"

"You're looking at it." The smile left his face. "Won't be much longer, though. Granny, she don't have many more years in her. When she goes, I'll be done."

"Where's she going to go?" Ezra asked, looking at the horse.

"She'll die sooner than later. It's a hard life for a horse, but she's done right by me, so I'll dig her a proper hole. There's some who don't, doncha know. I've seen it. The horse dies and they just leave them where they lay. The officials used to not say anything, but they're putting up a fuss now."

Ezra slid a glance toward Angus. "You're pretty old too, huh?"

"That I am, lad."

"So you'll die too?"

"Not today, probably not tomorrow either, but my day will come. Is gairid ár gcairt ar an saol seo."

Ezra tilted his head in question.

"Tis Gaelic. Our lease on life is short."

Ezra watched as Granny turned onto a different street without any prodding from Angus.

"She knows where to go?"

"Granny's been driving me home every day for the last twenty years."

Ezra counted his fingers, closed them, spread them once more, and counted again. "That's a lot of fingers."

"I see ye've had yourself a bit of education. Do ye miss school?"

"Oh, I never got to go to school. My sister did." Ezra gasped, realizing he'd mentioned his sister.

"There a problem with your sister, lad?" Angus asked, eyeing him.

"No, sir. It's just we—my brother and I—are not supposed to mention her on account of she ran away." Ezra thought about what Angus had said about knowing Tobias was alive. "My sister left over a year ago. She had a scar on her face. Did you see her?"

Angus was quiet for a moment. "Not that I can recall, but I've seen a lot of people over the years. If ye didn't go to school, who learned you?"

"My momma. She used to be a teacher before she married my papa." Talking about his parents made his stomach hurt. "Sir, if it's all the same to you, I'd rather not talk about my momma and papa right now."

"This too shall come to pass. There's nothing so bad that it couldn't be worse," Angus assured him.

Ezra didn't like the sound of that. He wouldn't want

to feel worse than he felt when he thought of never seeing his parents again. They rode in silence for a bit, Ezra staring in disbelief as the buildings gave way to open land. Suddenly Angus began to speak.

"Mr. Twomey gave me this jacket," Angus said, holding his sleeve in front of Ezra's face. "I'd been working for Mr. Maguire for some time and only had another couple weeks left on my contract. I was at the market with Darla—I used to escort her cause it wasn't proper for a lady to go out on her own. Anyway, Darla was haggling with a lady over some silks and I wasn't paying them no mind when, in the distance, I spy Mr. Twomey walking straight in my direction. I thought he was coming for me, but it turned out his new wife wanted some silks of her own. So I stayed back, talking to Mr. Twomey. I didn't want no part of him at first. He'd hurt me real bad the last time I saw him. But he seemed different. He asked about my life since leaving his care, and I told him. Then he said to me how he'd left the drink and how sorry he be for treating me the way he did. It was cold out and I didn't have a coat, so I shivered. The next thing I know, Mr. Twomey took this here jacket straight off his back and handed it to me. I thought he was being nice, but then he went and told me that he didn't much care for the thing. Said his wife was fond of the color, and beings she sewed it for him, he wore it.

"I started to tell him he should keep it, that I really didn't like it neither, but he insisted I should put it on. I'd no sooner done that than his wife came over and he told her I was the boy who'd helped him give up the drink. Imagine that? He said that to her, doncha know. I never did find out how I helped him, but his wife seemed to think I had something to do with it because she burst into tears, handed the babe to Mr. Twomey, and planted her lips right here on this cheek," he said, placing a finger to show the spot. "There weren't any snogging, just a simple kiss. But my Darla saw her and that didn't settle too well with her. Oh, she was polite about it until after they'd gone, but on the way home, she told me if I were going to marry her that there would be none of that—my kissing other ladies, that is. I started to tell her I wasn't the one doing the kissing when I realized what she'd said."

"What'd she say?"

"Why, she'd just said how she was going to marry me! I liked her well enough, but can you imagine my surprise when she said that?"

Ezra wasn't sure why getting married was a good thing, so he shook his head.

"Someday, you'll understand. But that wasn't even the best of it. It turns out Mr. Twomey had left a good bit of money in the pocket of this here jacket. Oh, I tried to find him so as to return it."

"You mean you were going to give the money back?"

"Oh, aye, it's better to be a man of character than a man of means, doncha know. But I couldn't find the man. Darla, she was a smart one; she told me we should consider it a wedding present. I thought that Mr.

Twomey might like that—him being so grateful to me and all. So we used the money to buy our first horse and cart. There's luck in this jacket. I tell you that 'cause I'd no sooner put it on than I had myself money in my pocket and a wife at my side. A heavy purse makes a light heart. Darla and I were happy."

Ezra wasn't sure if he thought having a wife to be lucky, but Angus seemed to think it was, so that was what mattered. He wondered if he too would have a wife someday. The thought had no sooner crossed his mind than he wrinkled his nose.

"What be troubling you, lad?"

"I don't think I want a wife."

"Not today, but there'll come a time. When ye do, find yourself a pretty one. An bhean atá dóighiúil is furasta a cóiriú. A handsome woman is easily dressed," he said, elbowing Ezra in the side.

Ezra returned Angus' smile. He couldn't recall the last time he'd felt this happy, not even when he was at home living with his momma and papa.

Chapter Eleven

Just as it began to rain, the buildings gave way to a series of small, freestanding shacks. With the shacks came a smell, much like the one in the stairway to the tenement building he'd once called home. Only this was much worse than anything he'd ever known. For a moment, Ezra thought he would heave as the awful smell of hordes of unwashed bodies compiled with human waste mingled with horse manure invaded his nostrils. He tried to hold his breath against the odor, but it was no use. The smell was everywhere.

A man leaning heavily on a crutch hobbled through the muddy street toward the cart. Ezra watched the pants leg flap against the wind as the fellow neared, and he realized it was empty. He moved quickly for a man with one leg, reaching the cart with ease.

Angus greeted him, then reached behind the buckboard and handed him some vegetables from the untouched basket. Several others joined them. Angus greeted each in turn, handing over a small offering from the basket. A lady with small children approached. Angus dug under the seat and pulled free a wrapped bundle he'd purchased shortly before leaving for the day.

She had tears in her eyes as he handed it down to her. He then gifted her with several hands full of vegetables.

While Ezra had seen his fair share of people wearing rags, he'd never in his life seen any to this degree. It further surprised him to discover their bodies to be as grungy as the rags upon their backs.

Immigrants. People from the boats…people his father had detested.

Though his momma fussed at papa for the way he spoke of them, she failed to tell him she too crossed the street to avoid them. Ezra lowered his eyes, hoping to avoid their stares.

After a few moments, Granny walked a few paces then turned into a tight alleyway. She walked a short distance then came to a stop in front of a weathered two-story shed.

"We'll be there, aye," Angus said, climbing from the cart.

"This is where you live?" Ezra asked, wrinkling his nose against the smell.

"Aye, it's not much to be sure, but it gives me a place to bring Granny in out of the weather." As he spoke, Angus unfastened the harnesses and leads. Once finished, Granny walked into the shed and nosed an empty pan.

Angus opened a bucket, scooped some oats into the pan, and scattered some fresh hay around the stall as Granny lowered her head to eat. Only after he'd gotten the horse settled did he move on to other tasks.

"Come here to me, lad," Angus said, returning to the cart. "Grab the other side and help Old Angus out."

The skies opened and Ezra hurried to do as told, lending a hand to maneuver the cart to the side of the building. Once they'd finished, Ezra followed the man back to the shed, only this time opening a side door and walking up the single flight of stairs. He opened a second door, flicking on a single overhead bulb, which flickered several times before finally staying on, though it did little to light the space, to reveal a single room. On one side, there was a bed and a wooden wardrobe. A tattered blue and yellow curtain hung from the ceiling, blocking off a small section. The other side of the room held a small kitchen complete with a stove and sink. A round table with two chairs separated the spaces.

Angus hung his hat upon a hook. He handed Ezra a towel then pushed the water from his clothes with his bare hands. He unlaced his boots, kicked them from his feet, then crossed to the table and removed his jacket, hanging it on the back of one of the chairs. Though the room appeared to be clean, the smell from outside permeated the space. Ezra wasn't sure if it was because the windows were open or because there were small holes in the floor. He felt certain that if he dropped to his knees and peered through one of the holes, he would be able to see Granny standing in her stall.

"The smell takes a bit to get used to." Angus chuckled. "By morning, you'll hardly notice it."

Ezra's eyes stung. He rubbed at his eyelids as if the

smell had somehow gotten inside. "How can you live here?"

Angus gave him a long look then slid a chair away from the table. Sitting, he gave a nod to the other chair and waited for Ezra to sit. As Ezra took his seat, Angus rose, walked to the far side of the room, and placed a bucket under a drip. Returning to his chair, he looked at Ezra. "It'll not be much, but at least ye have a roof over your head this night. There are many in the city that cannot say the same."

Ezra felt the sting of a blush creep up his face. "I'm sorry, sir, it's just that I've never smelled anything like it before."

"You'll be lucky for that, then. But that not be the whole of it, is it, lad?"

Ezra felt the blush deepen.

"Being prideful is one thing, but thinking yourself high and mighty is another. It can lead to a mighty hard fall. Most of the people we passed on the way in have very little, yet they are grateful to have that because it is theirs. And best ye be remembering they'll fight to keep it."

"Yes, sir," Ezra said in return.

"What do ye know about the people outside these walls?"

"Nothing, sir," Ezra said, looking at the floor.

"Why, I think ye be lying to me, lad. I can see it on that face of yours."

"They're immigrants," Ezra said, using the same

tone his father had when speaking of them.

"I take it your momma and papa did not come over on the boats?" If his tone had disturbed the man, he did not allow it to show.

"Oh no, sir," Ezra said, beaming with pride. "My papa and momma were Americans, born right here in the country."

Angus nodded. "That may be the truth, but I'd be willing to bet that their folks before them came over on the boats."

"Yes, sir. My momma used to tell my papa that whenever he talked about the people from the boats. She didn't like it when he called them cockroaches. But he'd remind her that those people were the ones who stole his job from him."

"Aye, I can see where that wouldn't sit right with a man. But a man is a man no matter where he's from. Your grandparents were immigrants. Now how would you feel if someone spat out their names the way you spit out the word as if it is acid on your tongue?"

Ezra shrugged. "I guess I wouldn't care much. I don't even know my grandparents. My momma's folks died before us kids were born and my papa's parents moved out west. I've never even met them. They wrote Papa a letter once asking for us to come. Papa said he'd have no part of it. It must have made Momma mad, as she and Papa had an awful fight about it."

Angus clamped his fingertips together, tapping them against his face in thought. "Do ye like me?"

"Yes, sir," Ezra said, bobbing his head. "I like you just fine."

"Remember what I told ye on the way over about me coming over on the boat?"

Ezra wrinkled his brow. "Yes, sir. But that was a long time ago."

"It doesn't matter how long I've lived here. I wasn't born here. When I arrived, some people looked at me the same way you looked at those folks we passed. Yes, I noticed." Angus jerked his thumb toward the door. "So did they. I didn't know what to expect when Mr. Twomey asked me if I wanted to come to America. I came because I had nothing better to do. But I heard many a story while crossing that mighty ocean, stories that would make a grown man cry. In fact, those doing the telling often had tears in their eyes. Some grew sick on the way over. Many died, their bodies tossed over the side so as not to make others sick. But never did I hear one of those men say they wished they hadn't come. No, sir, lad, those men and women were on their way to America because they'd heard all the stories of riches and land free for the taking. And you know what happened when they got here?"

"No, sir," Ezra said. He leaned closer, eager to hear of their fate.

"They were called names," Angus replied.

"What kind of names?"

"They were proud Irish men and Italians and a whole host of others. They were called names that would make your momma blush. But they came anyway, and do ye know why?"

Ezra shook his head.

"Because even as bad as things were for them here, it was far worse for them where they came from."

Ezra wrinkled his nose. "You mean it smelled worse than this?"

"It's not the smell I'm speaking of. The smell is because the city can't keep up with the number of people coming in looking for the promise of more. Your papa was mad because the immigrants took his job. But someday there will be others that come over and take the jobs of the men who took his. It's the way things are done."

Angus drummed his fingers on the table. "Do ye recall the man with the crutch?"

"The one missing his leg?"

"That be the one. He came over from Ireland. He'd barcly set foot on dry land when he got a job down at the docks. Happy as a clam he was for having found work straightaway. He got wedged between the dock and a ship and that's how he lost his leg. He could no longer work that job or pay his rent in the tenement, so he lives here."

Angus drummed his fingers once more. "Do ye recall the lady with the two wee lads and the baby in her arms?"

Ezra did recall them. Especially the way the oldest boy looked at him as if wishing he could trade places with him. "Yes."

"Her husband died before they reached America. She stepped off the boat not knowing anyone, nor being able to speak the language. She was with child, so she wasn't allowed to work. Now she has no one to care for her children if she could."

"Is that why you give them food?" It hadn't skipped Ezra's notice none of the people he spoke of had paid Angus for the food he'd given them.

"I don't give them anything," Angus replied.

"But I saw…"

"Ye didn't see anything 'cause ye was too busy trying not to. The man who lost his leg cleans out Granny's stall after I leave each day. In return, I bring him a few vegetables at the end of the day. The woman with the wee lads makes those meat pies that fill our stomachs each day. In return, I give her vegetables, a little meat, and supplies so that she can fill her and her lads' bellies as well. The others all do something in return for what I bring them each day. They do not wish to live this way, and pride keeps them from taking without giving in return."

"Do all of those people live here because they don't have jobs?"

"No, not all. Most just live here 'cause they have nowhere else to live or not enough money to help 'em find a better place."

"How long have you had your job?" Ezra asked.

"I've been selling my vegetables for over fifty years," Angus replied.

"How come no one ever took your job?"

Angus smiled. "When I started, there were only two vegetable men in the market, I being one of them. We stood selling our wares and there be land as far as the eye could see. Now ye can't look in any given direction without seeing a building, and more being built every day. I'll be long gone before I have to worry about not being able to make a living doing what I do. If I were a young man such as yourself trying to make it in this world, I'd keep going."

"Where would you go?"

"I guess I'd go out west and find me a bit of land where a man could stretch out a bit and smell air that was fit to breathe."

"You mean like where my grandparents went?"

"Perhaps. Are ye sure you don't recall where they live? I might be able to help you get to them if you do."

Ezra shook his head once more.

Angus sighed. "Well, you're here for now. I'll think on things and see what's to be done."

Ezra thought about what Angus said about the people he helped. He lifted his eyes and looked at him. "You want me to put my mark on the paper for you?"

Angus' eyes narrowed. For a moment, Ezra thought he was going to yell at him. Angus closed his eyes, and when he opened them, they were wet around the edges. "No, lad, you'll not be beholden to me. We've worked out a deal and I'll be paying ye for your help. But I'll never keep ye to it if ye find something better to do. Ye get a chance to make something of yourself, take it. Old Angus will wish you the luck of the Irish as ye be on your way. That set well with ye?"

"It does," Ezra agreed.

"Good, better be getting on to bed now. We'll be up before the dawn."

Ezra looked about the room, his eyes landing on the single bed. "Where will I sleep?"

"Tug one of the quilts off the bed and make a pallet on the floor. There's a pot for doing yer business behind that curtain over there. When you're finished, dump it out the window. Be mindful to dump it out the far window. If ye use this one, we'll be sure to step in it come morning."

Ezra did as told, then settled onto the floor, staring at the ceiling until darkness finally filled the room. As he listened to the rain pummel the ceiling, he knew the only thing that kept him from being one of the people he'd seen in the street was the man sleeping in the bed on the other side of the room. Angus said he didn't plan on dying today or tomorrow, but the man was older than anyone Ezra had ever known. As he drifted off to sleep, he wondered what would become of him when Angus was no longer there to look after him.

Chapter Twelve

"Lad, time to be up with ye," Angus called, waking him from his sleep.

Ezra opened his eyes. Squinting against the overhead light, he lay there listening as the rain beat a steady drum against the roof. Yawning, he stretched his arms wide. Though he had no bed, he realized that once he'd fallen asleep, he'd slept without waking. Maybe that was because it was the first time in a long time he'd actually felt safe. When living on the streets, he woke at every little noise thinking the gangs were about to grab him and tear him from limb to limb. Before that, it was his parents' fights that woke him, keeping him up most nights. He closed his eyes, squeezing them tight, wishing to be in his own bed. Not that he missed his parents' fights, but if he were indeed sleeping in his bed, it would mean they were not dead.

"Come on, lad. Fold that quilt and lay it on the end of my bed. Returning home looks best when the home ye return to is tidy," Angus said, pulling him from his thoughts.

Bringing the quilt with him, he folded the ends as he watched Angus slide a corn husk broom from side to side about the small room. Ezra placed the quilt on the bed and then went behind the curtain to relieve himself. Finishing, he took the pot to the far window, wrinkling his nose against the smell as he tilted the pot and watched the contents mingle with the soaking rain. His arm was wet when he pulled it inside.

"It's a fine day for young ducks," Angus said when Ezra turned from the window. "We'll best be getting to it. People still have to eat."

Ezra placed the pot in his other hand and wiped his arm on his shirt. He returned the pot to its place and turned to Angus for direction.

"Run next door and see Mrs. Duffy. She'll have our meat pies ready, aye."

Ezra slid a glance out the window. "Why, it's still dark out."

"Aye, she'll be up. Be mindful to keep your voice down so ye don't wake the wee ones, or Mrs. Duffy be likely to keep ye to look after them." Angus leaned the broom against the wall and walked to the wardrobe, pulled open a drawer, and withdrew a flat hat with a wide brim. "Come here to me, lad."

Ezra walked to where he stood and Angus placed the hat upon his head. It slid down over his face. Angus fiddled with it until it rested on the back of his head with the brim hovering just above his eyes.

Ezra let out a sigh. "It's too big."

"Aye, it is, but it'll help ye some," Angus said, returning to his broom. "Take the cloth from the counter.

Mrs. Duffy will be needing it to wrap the pies."

Ezra retrieved the cloth, then hurried down the stairs, the cap inching forward with each step. He opened the outer door, adjusting the hat as he stood staring out at the rain. The smell wasn't as bad as when he'd arrived. Ezra wondered if it was due to the rain or if, as Angus said, he'd grown used to it. *Best be out with ye.* He stepped out into the rain as Angus' voice sprang into his head. Though Mrs. Duffy only lived a few steps away, he was nearly soaked by the time he arrived at her door. He gave a quick knock, hunkering near the door as he waited for her to answer.

He was about to repeat the knock when the door opened, the smell of fresh-baked meat pies flooding his senses. Mrs. Duffy stood in the doorway, her dark hair illuminated by the dim light behind her. She was thin, her hair pulled away from her face, and she reminded him of his mother for the briefest of seconds. He was about to run to her when she spoke, yanking him back to reality.

"Ye'll be coming for the pies?" Though she spoke English, her accent was so strong, Ezra had to replay her words in his head before he answered.

He handed her the cloth. "Yes, ma'am."

She looked past him and motioned for him to enter. "It be a fine day for young ducks."

"That's what Angus said," Ezra told her as he entered. He removed his hat, shaking the excess water free before returning it to his head.

"Aye, it be an Irish saying." She pulled a towel from a hook near the door and handed it to him.

He used it to sop the water but stayed on the small rug near the entrance so as not to soil the floor with his wet feet. The shack of a house was much the same as the one Angus lived in, with wooden slats for walls and a single window on each end. Only Mrs. Duffy's home didn't have a second floor. The bed was larger, a good thing as all three of the children lay sleeping atop the covers, their limbs sprawled in all directions.

Mrs. Duffy saw him looking and smiled once again. "My older boy sleeps on the floor until I wake and lift him up and place him in my spot. It eases the mind to know he has a bed, if only for a while."

"I slept on the floor last night. It wasn't so bad."

"Ye didn't mind?"

"Oh, no, ma'am. I was just happy to be out of the rain."

She smiled then hurried to the stove. As she stood there with her back to him and the aroma of homemade cooking floating through the air, he once again thought of his mother and how much he missed her. He watched as she picked up a small cloth and pulled a tray from the oven. Setting the tray on the counter, she shook her hand and placed a finger into her mouth to soothe it.

It was then Ezra saw the stains on her dress and realized she wasn't wearing her apron. He pointed at her dress. "You forgot your apron."

A frown flitted across her face. She picked at the

stains, and he realized his mistake. The woman before him was not his mother. Not only that, but he'd embarrassed her. He knew it to be true, as he'd seen his mother act the same way whenever his father had asked why there was no more food on the table.

It was because there was no more to be had. Mrs. Duffy was not wearing an apron because she didn't have one to wear. He thought of the woman in his mother's kitchen and at how pleased she'd been when he'd allowed her to keep his mother's apron. He lowered his eyes to hide both the memory and his shame.

When he looked up once more, Mrs. Duffy had turned back to the stove, busying herself lifting the meat pies from the tray. A moment later, she returned to him, handing him the cloth containing the meat pies. Tightly wrapped, it was still warm to the touch. Her smile was gone. Her eyes held the humiliation he'd thrust upon her. His heart ached, knowing it was he who'd stripped her of her joy.

I am my father's son.

He hadn't meant to embarrass her, but he wasn't sure she would understand if he were to tell her that, for a moment, she'd reminded him of his mother. He opened his mouth thinking to apologize, but she shook her head.

"You must go before you wake the boys," she said, glancing toward the bed.

He stuffed the meat pies into his pocket to keep them from getting wet, adjusted his hat once more, and stepped out into the warm rain as she gently closed the door behind him.

Gone was the smell of his mother's kitchen, replaced by the stench of the city. He sloshed through the mud mindless of the rain, only realizing he was crying as he neared the shack he now called home. He paced back and forth, trying to quell the tears. When they finally ceased, he wiped his face with the tail of his shirt. It was then he realized that, in his distress, he'd managed to cover himself in the filth that surrounded the shacks. Now he too looked like the others he'd turned his nose up at only the day before. *We are all the same.*

He met Angus coming down the stairs.

Angus raised an eyebrow upon seeing him, but if he saw Ezra's distress, he did not make mention of it. "I thought maybe you'd gotten lost. We'll go hitch up Granny. I expect she'll be waiting for us. Push that hat back on your head so ye don't trip in the mud."

Ezra adjusted the hat and led the way to Granny's stall. The horse tossed her head and snorted a greeting the moment they entered.

Used to seeing her with her head down looking sad, Ezra pointed at the mare. "She looks happy."

"Oh, aye. Granny is always happy to see me. I think it is because the lass knows I'm old and is worried about who will feed her if I fail to wake one day," Angus said, pulling the harness from the hook.

Ezra felt his anxiety grow. He didn't like it when Angus spoke of dying, especially since he didn't know what would become of him if he didn't have the man watching over him. Ezra thought of Mrs. Duffy and wondered if she would take him in. Not likely after how he'd made her sad. Besides, if not for Angus, neither she nor the others would have any food.

"Granny's not the only one who counts on you. What would happen to Mrs. Duffy and the others if you were to die?" Ezra wished to include himself in the question but decided against it. Truthfully, he didn't want to know.

"I'll do what I can while I can. After I'm gone, they'll either figure things out or die." Angus said, fastening the last harness in place. "Throw open that door, lad."

"Doesn't it bother you?" Ezra asked, pushing the door open.

"I didn't get to be an old man by worrying about things I cannot change," Angus said as he led Granny from the stall. He looked to the sky and smiled. "The rain be gone by the time we reach the docks."

"How can you tell?"

"The knowing also comes with age," Angus said with a wink. "Don't ye fret about growing old, lad. There are worse things in life that can happen to ye than dying."

"I guess so," Ezra said, following Angus up into the cart. "Are you not a little scared of dying?"

Angus gave Granny her lead. "There is an Irish proverb that goes: May the good earth be soft under you when you rest upon it, and may it rest easy over you when, at the last, you lay out under it. And may it rest so lightly over you that your soul may be out from under it quickly, and up and off, and be on its way to God."

Ezra wasn't sure what it meant, but he liked the way Angus smiled when he said it. "You know a lot of Irish sayings, don't you, Angus?"

"Aye, the Irish, it be in me blood. I expect it be in yours as well," Angus replied.

"Does that mean I can say those things too?"

"I expect ye hang around old Angus long enough, and you'll pick up a thing or two," Angus said as he settled back against the wooden seat.

Ezra followed the man's lead, resting against the back of the bench. As they rode along in compatible silence, Ezra prayed that Angus would live long enough to teach him the ways of the Irish.

Chapter Thirteen

The rain lingered late into the day, only subsiding as the contents of the baskets dwindled. The dreary conditions did little to improve Ezra's mood. His guilt of the morning weighed heavy on him and had rekindled his grief over losing his momma. On more than one occasion, he'd thought he saw her, only to have the woman disappear into a crowd of bystanders. Once, he'd nearly called out her name before remembering she was not alive to hear his shouts. "What's eating at ye, lad? You've been brooding all day," Angus said as Ezra sat staring out into the crowd of late-afternoon shoppers.

Ezra didn't wish to tell him of his grief. Nor did he want to admit to his indiscretion of the morning.

"Come on, lad, out with it," Angus prodded.

"Sir? Did you really mean what you said about putting aside a bit of money for me each day?" He hadn't intended to ask for any money, but it was the only way he could figure to ease his guilt.

Angus slid a glance sideways. "Aye, I did. Decided to take your leave, did you?"

Ezra shook his head. "Oh, no, sir. I like working for ye...I mean you, just fine. I just wondered if I could maybe have some of it."

Angus looked to make sure no one was near; then, turning his back to the road, he pulled a thick wad of bills from the inside of his jacket pocket. Had he known how to whistle, Ezra would have done just that. Instead, he swallowed and stared his disbelief.

"How much do you need, lad?"

Ezra felt his eyes grow wide. "You mean to tell me I've earned all of that?"

Angus chuckled. "Not even close. But I figure if ye had reason to ask for it, you'd have a mighty good reason."

"Yes, sir. I do. I wish to buy an apron," Ezra replied.

Angus' brows knitted together, and for a moment, Ezra thought the man would deny his request. Instead, Angus pulled a bill from the stack and handed it to him.

"This should be enough to buy ye a fine apron. There's a lady down the end of the street that sells em. However, I don't know if she'll be having any left yet today. We are nearly finished here. Go on and run down there and see. If she don't have any left, then ye tell her you'll be back in the morning, and can she save one special. If she balks, just tell her I sent you. Oh, and put that bill in your front pocket and make sure not to let anyone bump into you. Dirty buggers will steal it from ye before you reach the end of the street if ye let 'em."

Ezra was off, sloshing through the fresh mud, smiling as it squished its way in between his toes. By the time he reached the wagon with the aprons, he looked as grungy as some of the folks he'd seen near Angus' house.

The woman selling aprons was speaking with a man wearing a neat black suit and tall hat. She took one look at him and shooed him away with her hands. "Go on, you filthy little urchin. You'll not be stealing from me today. Back away before you soil my aprons."

Ezra pulled the bill from his pocket and waved it at the woman. "I'll not be stealing from you. I've got money."

The man who'd been watching everything turned to address the woman. "Why, Mrs. Rouse, it seems as if you have this fellow pegged wrong. He's a paying customer and should be treated as such."

"I'll treat him all right as long as he don't get mud on anything," she replied. "Now, what color are you looking for, and your mother, is she a large woman or small?"

He hadn't thought about the color. Nor did he know what his mother had to do with it. He took a step closer so he could get a better look.

"That'll be far enough," the woman bellowed.

"Really, Madam, you would not be speaking that way if it were a man standing before you," the man in the suit interjected.

"I would too if he were covered in mud," she barked.

Ignoring her, the man turned to him, bending to meet his eye. "Are you looking for an apron for your mother, son?"

"No, sir. My momma's dead." Ezra's voice cracked as he answered.

"I'm sorry to hear that." The man's face was sincere in his apology. "Let's try this a different way. Who are you purchasing the apron for?"

Ezra wasn't sure why it mattered, but he didn't see the harm in telling. "It's for the nice lady who makes me and Mr. Angus our meat pies. She doesn't have one, and her dress is mighty soiled."

"Angus?" The woman sounded nicer this time.

"Yes, ma'am. That's the man I work for. I live with him."

"You do?" She seemed surprised to hear this.

"Yes, ma'am. I earned this here money from him, and I aim to use it to buy Mrs. Duffy a fine apron."

The lady narrowed her eyes. "And just who is this Mrs. Duffy?"

"The lady who makes us meat pies," Ezra repeated. The man in the hat snickered. But Ezra didn't know what he found so funny.

"Now that we have that straight, are you going to sell the boy an apron or not?" The man's tone was more serious now. "If not, I will steal him away and he can buy one from me."

Ezra looked up at the man in the fancy suit. "You sell aprons?"

"My store does," the man replied.

"Imagine that, a whole store just for aprons," Ezra mused.

The man chuckled. "We sell a great many things, aprons being one of them."

"Don't you go trying to steal my customer. The boy came here first," the woman said, holding up a pale blue ruffled apron. "Now, how do you like this one, boy?"

Ezra looked at the apron and could almost picture his momma wearing it. He smiled, knowing she would look pretty in that color.

"So this is the one, then?" she asked, sounding pleased with herself.

He recalled his mother's old stained apron. It was simple and white, or at least it had been so at one point in time. But it was thick and kept his mother's clothes from getting stained. And even covered with stains, the woman who now cooked in his mother's kitchen seemed very pleased to get it. "No, ma'am. I think I'd just like a plain white one."

Mrs. Rouse huffed and mumbled something under her breath as she reached into a covered basket and removed a crisp white apron. While plain, it appeared thicker and looked much like the one his momma had used.

Ezra nodded his head and offered her the bill. She took it and handed him a few coins in return.

"You don't expect the boy to carry it home like that, do you," the man in the hat asked as she started to hand Ezra the apron.

The woman huffed once more before placing it on a piece of brown paper, folding it closed, and then tying it with a string. The man nodded his approval as she handed Ezra the paper.

"Hold up there, son. Let me walk with you a way," the man in the hat said as Ezra turned to leave. The man tipped his hat to the woman before turning his attention back to Ezra. "Come this way. The mud will be less on the sidewalk."

Ezra followed him from the street, wondering why the man would wish to walk with him. He got his answer when next the man spoke.

"You'll recall I told you I have a department store?"

"Yes, sir."

"I was wondering if you'd like to come work for me?"

"Oh, no, sir."

The man turned his head in surprise. "You wouldn't?"

"No, sir," Ezra repeated. "I like working for Mr. Angus. He doesn't wear a fancy suit, but I like him just fine."

The man chuckled. "That's what I thought. You see, I could tell that you are a compassionate, trustworthy fellow, and I need your sort around my store."

"Why, I'm just a boy," Ezra said, stating the obvious. "There are lots of boys on the street."

"Yes, but most boys prefer to steal what they wish to have. I see it every day; however, it's not often I see a boy such as yourself spending his hard-earned money on someone else," the man explained.

"I don't need any money just now, and Mrs. Duffy sure could use this apron," Ezra replied.

"And that is precisely why I wanted to extend the offer. I'll tell you what, if your fortune ever changes and you find yourself in need of a job, you ask someone how to get to B. Altman & Company on Fifth Avenue. Think you can remember that?"

"I'll try, sir."

The man stopped and held up a finger for Ezra to do the same. He reached into his pocket, pulled out a card, and handed it to him. "Take this card. You find yourself in need of a job, come to my store, and I'll see to it myself."

"Aren't you coming?" Ezra asked when the man started to walk away.

"No, son, this is where we part ways. You make sure to hang on to that card," he said firmly.

"I will, sir," Ezra promised. He shoved the card into the pocket with his change and watched the man for several seconds before continuing on his way.

Angus was placing the board on the end of the cart when he returned. He looked up when Ezra approached and nodded toward the package Ezra held. "Did ye find what you were looking for, then?"

"Yes, sir," Ezra replied.

Angus looked toward the sky and frowned.

"Is it going to rain again?" Ezra asked, following his gaze.

"No, we'll not be so lucky this evening," Angus said with a sigh.

"Lucky? Why, I thought you were tired of the rain."

"I am, but it would help to wash some of that grub off ye now, wouldn't it, lad?"

Ezra looked at his clothes. "My momma would not be pleased if she saw me like this, and my papa, he'd…"

"Not to worry, lad, we'll see ye get yourself clean," Angus assured him. "Now, tell me, who'd you buy that apron for if ye don't mind me asking?"

"I got it for Mrs. Duffy," Ezra said without looking at him.

"Did you now? And why would you go and do a thing like that?"

"Cause I made her sad." He wanted to add that she reminded him of his mother but decided against it. Only once he started talking, he couldn't seem to stop. "I asked her why she wasn't wearing her apron. I didn't mean nothing by it. I saw that her dress was stained and thought to remind her she'd forgot to put her apron on. Then I saw her face. I've seen my momma's face look like that before, so I knew. I tried to tell her I was sorry, that I didn't mean nothing by it, but she told me to go, and I'm afraid she won't make us any more meat pies."

"Meat pies, eh? Is that the real reason ye bought it for her?"

Ezra slid a glance toward Angus. "No, sir."

"Out with it, lad."

Ezra's lip trembled.

"Ain't no harm ever came from crying," Angus assured him.

The words had no sooner left Angus' mouth than

Ezra burst into tears, crying until, at last, he had no more tears to spill.

"There, now. Feel better, do ya?"

Ezra nodded.

"Good. Now tell me the cause of 'em."

"When Mrs. Duffy opened the door, it was still dark out. And being such, she reminded me of my momma." Ezra sniffed. "Then she spoke to me and sounded like you, only worse. I mean, I could barely understand her, so she didn't remind me of my momma anymore. Then she turned around and the smells coming from the stove, I don't know. It happened again. When she faced me once more, I saw my momma and that her dress was ruined. So I asked her where her apron was, and it made her sad."

Angus gave him a hard look. "That's not the all of it."

"No, sir. Before my momma died, I saw that her apron was a mess. Not dirty, mind you, but stained. I thought that one day I would get myself a proper job and promised I would buy her a new apron." Ezra swallowed. "I never got to buy my momma that apron."

Angus nodded his understanding. "You've got yourself a problem, son. Mrs. Duffy, she's a proud woman. She'll not let ye be giving her something without giving you something in return."

"She won't?"

"No, lad. As I said, she's a proud lass."

"Why, she gave me meat pies just this morning,"

Ezra reminded him.

"She did at that, but she did it because she and I have an arrangement. We have to use our smarts," Angus said, tapping Ezra on the head. As he did, Ezra's hat fell forward, covering his eyes. Angus smiled. "That's it."

"What's it? Ezra asked, pushing the hat out of his eyes.

"When she makes a fuss about how she cannot accept the apron, you make sure that hat falls over your face. Then you comment as to how you wish you knew someone who could fix it for ye."

Ezra removed the hat from his head, turning it in his hands. "Do you think it will work?"

"It'll work. Mrs. Duffy might be proud, but she's no stupid. She'll know what ye are up to and probably figure who put you up to it. But she's a woman, and women like pretty things. Now come, lad, we best be getting home before the fog rolls in."

Ezra looked up at the clear sky then began collecting the empty baskets. "Sir," he said when they finished loading all the baskets. "If you have all that money, why do you not live in one of the fancy buildings in town?"

Angus climbed onto the bench seat and waited for Ezra to join him before answering. "The wife and I had a fine house across the Hudson River. When she passed, I just couldn't see myself living there all alone. Granny here was getting on in years, and I thought to move closer, so she didn't have to walk so far."

"But why not live in one of the better buildings?"

Ezra asked once more.

"Better for who? Me or Granny?" Angus asked. "Where we live gives her plenty of room. She wouldn't have that if we lived closer. Sometimes a man has to think of more than himself. Just like ye did today."

"I did?"

"Sure enough. You could have used that money to buy you a new hat, but you put your needs aside and helped out someone less fortunate. That's a fine quality in a man."

"But I'm not a man."

"Son, you are more of a man than a lot of fellows I know. More than that, your momma would be proud of you for what ye did today. Your papa too. And if you don't mind me saying so, I'm mighty proud to call you my friend."

Ezra blushed. While he was pleased to make Angus happy, a part of him wondered how long it would last. There was a time when his papa had uttered the same words.

***

Freshly scrubbed and wearing his spare set of clothes, Ezra carefully picked his way across the muddy path to Mrs. Duffy's door. True to Angus' words, a heavy blanket of fog cloaked the morning sky. Ezra thought of the night he'd left home, the skin on the back of his neck prickled, and he broadened his steps. He found the door, rapped his knuckles against the wood, and waited for it to open.

Mrs. Duffy opened the door, smiling at the sight of him. She wore the apron he'd given her the night prior. Though no longer pristine, it looked nice. She must have seen the approval in his face as her smile stretched to her eyes.

"You've come for the meat pies?" she said, moving aside to allow him entrance.

"And my hat too, if you please," he said with a grin. He handed her the cloth for the pies, his stomach growling as she moved to the stove. Even from where he stood on the other side of the room, he heard her contented sigh as she grabbed the thin towel with the bottom of her apron and pulled the tray from the oven without getting burned. She placed two meat pies in the cloth, folded it tight, and returned to him. As he put them into his pocket, she reached behind him, retrieved his hat from the hook on the wall, and handed it to him.

He saw the moisture in her eyes as she watched him settle it onto his head. Not wishing to ruin the moment, he turned and walked into the fog, only this time, he did so without fear.

Chapter Fourteen

July 14, 1919

Ezra woke to voices, agitated and yelling somewhere in the distance. He opened his eyes, surprised to see sunshine flooding in through the open windows. He instantly knew something was amiss. *Has something happened to Angus?* He scrambled to his feet, relief washing over him as he heard the man's voice among the others. While relieved to know his friend to be okay, an ominous fear continued to spread through him. In the four years he'd been working for the man, Angus had never let him sleep through the morning, nor had they missed leaving for the market before the dawn of the day.

Ezra hurried to fold the quilt setting it on Angus' bed before heading out to see why he hadn't rousted him. As he opened the door, a stab of grief raced through him as he saw the reason for the delay. A group of men stood with their backs to him, each pulling on thick ropes while hoisting Granny's lifeless body onto a flat wagon.

She's dead.

Ezra stood in the doorway for several moments, trying to get his emotions under control. He was eleven years old, much too old to be seen crying over a dead animal. She was only a horse after all. Not true; she was not merely a horse. She was the only thing that kept him from a life on the streets. Angus had made that clear from the start. While true, Ezra realized he was currently more upset by her death than what her demise meant to him. He sniffed, wiped the tears from his eyes, and walked to where Angus stood watching as the men carefully lowered Granny onto the wagon.

"She'll be walking on roads of gold with nay a harness from now on," Angus said by way of greeting. "I woke in the night and knew she was slipping over. I don't know how I knew. I just did. I went down and sat with her while she passed. These men are going to see about burying her. I'm going with them to see it gets done. You're welcome to come, but don't think ye have to if you have something better to do."

It was the first time Ezra could recall that Angus didn't assume him to be going with him. Ezra recalled Angus' words the first day he had brought him home. *I'll give you work as long as there's work to be had. When Granny dies, I'll need ye no more.* Ezra swallowed his fear. "I want to go with you. Granny was my friend too."

Angus smiled and turned back to the others without another word.

***

It took several hours to reach their destination and nearly double that for the men to dig a hole deep enough for Angus' satisfaction. After lowering Granny into the ground and packing it with dirt, the men stepped away,

110

"There are several around the city run by The Children's Aid Society. Lodging houses that will give ye a bed and a meal for a small price. I've seen many mentions of them in the newspaper over the years. They have a program you might want to look into."

Ezra slid a glance toward Angus. "What kind of program?"

"They'd put ye on a train and ship you out west. It must be working out, as they've done it plenty over the years."

"Out west? What would I do when I got there?"

"Work on a farm. Find yourself a new family."

You are the only family I need and you're sending me away. Ezra narrowed his eyes. "I don't need a new family. Families ain't nothing but trouble."

"You don't have to agree to be sent out west, but I'd feel better if I didn't have to worry about ye living on the streets. Tell me you'll give it a try."

It wasn't as if he had another option. "I guess."

The remainder of the trip back passed mostly in silence. Ezra found it difficult to speak without fear he'd break out into sobs begging Angus to let him stay. When at last they reached Angus' house, Ezra leapt from the wagon, racing up the stairs without waiting for the man. By the time Angus had thanked the men for helping with Granny, Ezra had already washed up in the sink, changed into his extra set of clean clothes, and had shoved the few belongings he had acquired into the only thing that remained of his prior life. While he had long outgrown his clothes, he still held on to the pillowcase his mother had made for him.

Upon seeing him standing there pillowcase in hand, Angus paused. Recovering quickly, he stepped inside and placed his hat on the hook. "Do you have everything?"

Ezra's heart sank. For a moment, he thought the man about to reconsider sending him away. "Yes, sir."

"Ye can stay this one more night. It's late in the day, and they may have trouble finding a bed for you tonight."

"Okay," Ezra said, neglecting to add he'd had every intention of asking Mrs. Duffy if he could spend the night sleeping on her floor instead.

Angus went to the small table, pulled a chair free, and sat. "I guess ye be pretty sore with me about now?"

I sure am. "A little."

"You'll be thinking to stop by Mrs. Duffy's and ask if ye can live with her now."

"How'd you know that?" Ezra blurted.

Angus laughed. "Because it's what I would do."

Ezra joined him at the table. "You would?"

"Sure I would, if I was in your shoes." Angus gave him a hard stare. "Don't do it."

"Why not? She's nice enough," Ezra replied.

"She is, and she'd agree to let ye stay."

"She would?" Ezra couldn't hide the relief in his words.

"Don't ye do it, lad," Angus repeated. "You cross that woman's threshold, and it won't be for a night or even a year. Why, if you stay, you'll grow old there festering in this rot with the rest of them. You're better than that, boy."

Ezra was shocked. Angus had always told him they were all the same. "But you said…"

"I know what I said. And I mean it. You ain't better than any of those people. We are all the same, but some people reach for more while others are content on living in a shack their whole lives."

Ezra knew Angus to be speaking of himself. "But you had a reason for staying."

"Yes, and now that reason is dead and buried. And do ye know what I'm going to do?"

"What?"

"Nothing. I'm going to stay right here until I die."

"Then I can stay with you."

"NO!" Angus said, slamming his fist on the table. Ezra jumped and Angus relaxed his hand. "Listen to me, lad. You have to get out of here. If ye are still here when I die, you'll still be here the day you die. You are young. If I was your age, I'd gladly hop on one of those trains. I wish I'd been given the chance. I want ye to have a better life. Please don't let me down. More than that, don't let your mother down."

"My mother?"

"Do ye think she'd be happy knowing ye are living here?"

Ezra shook his head.

"Then if you won't do it for me, do it for her. You

might not be able to buy her a new apron, but if she is looking down upon you this day, ye can find yourself a life that would make her proud."

Ezra hadn't thought of it like that. Angus' words were true. His mother would be heartbroken if she knew where he was living. Taking a deep breath, he pulled himself taller in the chair. "I'll go. I might not like it much, but I'll go."

"That's a good lad, son. You'll get by alright, I can promise you that."

"How can you be sure when you are not going to be there to help me?"

Angus gave him a long look before answering. "Because I'm going to send ye off with my lucky jacket. If you'll no be ashamed to wear it."

Ezra raised his brows in surprise. In all the years he'd known him, he had never known the man to leave the house without the jacket. Angus must really want him to be safe if he was willing to give it to him. "You're not fooling me, are you?"

Angus laughed. "No, lad, I'm not fooling you. But you'll have to wait until the morn, so I have time to clean it and mend it a bit."

Ezra studied the jacket. He didn't see where it needed mending. He decided that maybe that was Angus' way of holding on to it a bit longer, so he nodded his agreement.

"Good. Then I'll see to supper. I'm afraid Mrs. Duffy will no be making it for us this day."

Ezra felt his excitement wane. "Because we didn't bring vegetables and meat back, right?"

"That's right."

"Angus, what will happen to the people you help?"

"Don't you worry about that, lad, we'll work out a new arrangement. As long as I'm here, I won't let my friends starve."

"But what after that?" Ezra pressed.

"I've got some time yet, lad. We'll figure things out," Angus promised.

"Maybe I should leave the jacket with you," Ezra said softly.

"Don't you worry about my luck. I've got the luck of the Irish with me, and if I'm right in my suspicions, I believe ye to have it as well."

"Do you really think so?"

"I do, but just to be safe, you can wear the jacket for a while. Not forever like this old fool, but ye wear it until you find ye luck and a bit longer if you like," Angus said.

"How will I know when it's time to take it off?" Ezra asked.

Angus smiled a sly smile. "When ye have enough money in your pocket to buy yourself a spot of land, you'll know it's time to retire the jacket."

"I'll be wearing it until I'm as old as you," Ezra sighed.

Angus stood and ruffed Ezra's hair. "I think you'll find your luck sooner than that. Until then, this jacket will suit ye well enough. It's too good to throw away, too ugly for anyone to wish to steal, and breathes well enough to keep ye cool in the summer and warm in the winter."

Ezra blew out a whistle. "Then it really is a magical coat."

"That it be, lad. That it be. Why, I wouldn't be surprised if it brings ye luck the first time ye wear it," Angus said with a wink.

Ezra wasn't so sure about the luck, but he knew that wearing it would make him feel better on any account.

Chapter Fifteen

Tuesday, July 15, 1919

Riding in the taxi should have been the greatest experience in his life, as Ezra had never ridden in a motorcar. However, his heart was so full of sorrow, it overshadowed the event. By the time the taxi pulled to the curb in front of the luxury department store, Ezra was trembling from head to toe. The driver stepped out and opened the door for Angus, who motioned for Ezra to follow.

"Come along, lad," Angus said as he handed the driver some money.

Ezra looked at the massive building, which counted seven windows high, including the window over the door, and stretched all the way to the next block, and gulped. "Why, I'll get lost in there!"

"Not to worry, lad. You're a smart one. You'll do just fine," Angus said, leading the way inside. As they entered, a tall man in a dark suit rushed to greet them.

The man eyed Angus' coat. "May I be of service to you gentlemen?"

Angus handed the man Ezra's card. "We're looking for this fellow."

"Indeed," the man said, eyeing them once more. "Is he expecting you?"

"Probably a lot sooner than now," Angus replied.

"If you'll wait here…"

"I'll take it from here, Mr. Dickinson."

Ezra looked up to see the man who had given him the card. Though he wasn't wearing the tall hat, he was certain it was the same man.

"Colonel Friedsam," the man said, extending his hand to both Ezra and Angus in turn. "You can call me Colonel."

Ezra blew out a whistle. "You own this whole store?"

"Wouldn't it be splendid if I did? No, I'm but part of the Altman Foundation," the man replied.

"Does that mean you can't give me a job?" Ezra wasn't sure if the thought made him happy or sad.

Colonel Friedsam laughed. "Is that what brought you in here?"

"Yes, sir. You told me if I ever wanted a job, I should come see you," Ezra reminded him.

Colonel Friedsam tilted his head to get a better look. "The boy with the apron?"

"Yes, sir," Ezra said, smiling for the first time since they'd entered.

The man rocked back on his heels. "I must say you clean up rather well. If I recall, when last we spoke, you were caked with mud."

"Well, it had been raining."

"So it had," he agreed, then turned his attention to

Angus. "And you, sir, are you a relative?"

"No, sir, just a friend. The lad's been working for me for a number of years, and well, my horse died and I'll not be needing his help any longer," Angus replied.

Ezra bit his lower lip to keep from crying.

"I see," the Colonel said, returning his attention to Ezra. "Just what kind of work do you have in mind?"

"Gee, Mister, I don't know. You're the one who told me I should come see you."

"So I did," the man said, massaging his chin. "Do you know your way around the kitchen? We have an entire Charleston plantation on the eighth floor. Serves the most divine cuisine. You should check it out when we are finished, my treat."

Ezra didn't know what either cuisine or a Charleston plantation was, but he was surprised to discover the building to have eight floors. "I counted seven windows."

"Yes, some of the windows are double, which can be rather deceiving."

"Oh, and I know my way around Angus' kitchen," Ezra said, answering the original question.

"My house is but a humble home," Angus replied.

"Yes, of course," Colonel Friedsam said with a nod. "How about we start you out as a doorman until we find something more suitable?"

"What's a doorman?" Ezra asked.

"Just what it sounds like," Colonel Friedsam replied. "You will stand at the front door and open it for our customers."

Ezra laughed. "And you'll pay me for that?"

"Oh, to be sure, and sometimes the gentlemen will give you a coin or two."

"For what?"

"For opening the door."

Ezra frowned. "I thought you were going to pay me."

Colonel Friedsam smiled. "Not to worry, you'll get paid. We shall also furnish you with a uniform."

"What's a uniform?"

"You'll get a nice pair of knickers and a jacket to go with it."

"Oh," Ezra said, nodding his understanding. "You don't have to give me a jacket. Angus is going to give me the one he's wearing. I promised I would not take it off until I have enough money in my pocket to buy me some land."

"Oh, my," Colonel Friedsam said in return.

Ezra wasn't sure, but he thought the man looked as if he would be ill.

***

"I don't think he likes your jacket," Ezra said once they'd climbed into another taxi.

Angus chuckled. "No, but he told ye that you can wear it. I told ye it would bring ye some luck. We even got a free meal. Why, I haven't eaten like that since the missus passed."

"My momma was a fine cook, but she never cooked anything like that."

122

"Aye, she would if she had had the resources."

All this talk of his mother reminded Ezra of his current predicament. "Maybe if I put the jacket on now, you won't make me go to the Lodging House."

"Now, enough of that, lad. We had this out last eve. Why, you can't hold the doors for fine people of the city if you smell like you live in a horse barn."

"Granny's dead!" Ezra said, regretting the harshness of his words the moment they passed his lips.

"Aye, that she is, but the place will smell just as bad all the same." Angus shrugged out of his coat and brushed at the sleeves. "Here, put this on, lad. It's only a short ride and we'll have ye ready when we get there."

Ezra hurried to put it on, excited to finally get to wear it. He sighed his disappointment when the jacket proved too big.

"You'll grow into it," Angus said, rolling up the sleeves.

Ezra felt a fullness under his right arm. "It feels strange."

Angus pushed his hand away. "Remember I told ye I had to mend it? I stuffed a bit of paper in there so the hole wouldn't show."

"Maybe you should have just left it."

"Pay it no mind. Ye will get used to it. I tell ye what, anytime you feel it a-buggering you, you think of me. That way, you'll never forget me."

"I don't want to go." Ezra sniffed. He'd promised himself he wouldn't cry, so he turned and looked out the window, amazed at how fast the buildings passed by. Much faster than riding while Granny pulled the cart. The thought of the horse lying in the hole did him in. Tears rolled down his cheeks like rain as he wondered for the hundredth time if his parents were also covered with dirt. When the taxi pulled to the corner, Ezra was surprised to see that he was not the only one crying. "Don't cry, Angus. I'll never forget you. I promise."

"Nor I ye," Angus said, wiping the moisture from his eyes. "Stick ye hand in the pocket."

Ezra did as he said and pulled out several bills along with a few coins. "You forgot your money."

"No, lad, it belongs to you. Ye earned it. You keep the coins and then give the fellow in there the rest. It will pay for your board until ye start earning a wage. And ye mind that jacket. Don't you let anyone take it from ye," Angus said firmly.

"I won't."

"Good. Ye be a good lad, then, and be on your way. Wouldn't be good for us to stay out here blubbering all day."

Ezra got out and walked toward the building. Halfway up the stairs, he turned to wave a final farewell. He lifted his hand and managed a trembling smile. Angus tipped his hat in return. Ezra took two steps, his legs feeling like he was trudging through mud. He stopped, thinking to run down the steps and beg Angus not to leave him. When he turned, the taxi was gone.

***

Friday afternoon, July 18, 1919

Ezra stood by the door, eagerly awaiting the next customer. He was still amazed to be getting paid to open a door. He'd only worked at the store for three days and had already earned two whole dollars in tips. One lady gave him a quarter to carry her packages to the taxi, and a short man with a hearty laugh gave him double that for having the courage to wear what he referred to as an atrocious jacket. Though Ezra didn't know what the word meant, he thought the man must have liked the jacket to have tipped him that much. A woman in a dress short enough to see her knees had kissed him on the cheek and rubbed her hand upon his head for good luck.

A lady leading a large white dog approached and stood waiting for Ezra to open the door. Ezra gaped at the dog, which had long thin legs with balls of fur just above its feet and at the end of the tail.

"Come along, Fifi," the woman said when the dog paused to sniff Ezra's jacket.

"It's okay, ma'am, he probably just smells Granny." Ezra ran his hand across the dog's fur. "Wow, his fur is so soft."

"'She' is a poodle. They have hair, not fur. Fifi, do leave that boy alone." She tugged at the dog's leash. "Fifi never pays me that much attention. What kind of perfume does your Granny use?"

"Oh, Granny doesn't use perfume. She's a horse. Or at least she was. She died a few days ago. I saw a dog in the market eating horse poop covered with flies. There were a lot of flies when we buried Granny. Maybe your dog likes the smell of them."

The woman's eyes went wide. "She most assuredly does not," she said, pulling the dog into the store.

"I see you are making friends, Ezra."

Ezra looked to see Colonel Friedsam standing behind him. "Oh, I don't think that lady is my friend. Her dog just liked my jacket."

"So I heard. It might be best not to make mention of Granny while you are here. Our customers don't like to be bothered by things such as dying horses."

"Oh, I don't think it was the fact that Granny died that bothered her. I think she didn't like that her dog likes flies."

Colonel Friedsam bit at his bottom lip. "Yes, well, perhaps we shall not mention the flies either. Are you enjoying your work?"

"Yes, sir, but I don't know why you call it work. All I do is open the door," Ezra said.

"Yes, but I assure you the people you open the door for are mighty appreciative."

"Maybe, but you could save a lot of money if you made everyone go in and out the same door. Then you wouldn't need to pay so many people to open them."

"Perhaps, but if we did that, then you and the other doormen would be out of a job," Colonel Friedsam reminded him. "You wouldn't like that very much now, would you?"

"No, sir, I guess I wouldn't."

"So you do like working here?"

"Course I do."

"Splendid. Collect your paycheck and I'll see you back here in two days."

"Two days? Did I do something wrong?"

"Wrong? Oh, no, not at all. We are closed on Saturday and Sunday. Benjamin, the original owner, had strict rules against having Saturday hours. He likes the employees to be able to spend more time with their families," Colonel Friedsam assured him. Ezra frowned and the man realized his mistake. "How are you getting on with the boys at the Lodging House?"

"Okay, I guess."

"Are you not happy there?"

Ezra considered telling the man he'd not made any friends thus far. But then he'd have to admit he hadn't even tried. The truth of the matter was he didn't know how to make friends. He'd never really been around anyone his age except Anastasia and Tobias, and they were his siblings, so they had to be his friends. For the last four years, Angus and Granny had been his only friends. Granny was dead and Angus no longer wished to be his friend. Now the only person he knew was standing before him, but though the man was nice, Ezra didn't consider him a friend. He decided to answer with a partial truth. "Oh yes, sir, I have a hot meal every night and a real bed to sleep in. The roof don't leak and the place doesn't smell, well, not that bad anyway."

Colonel Friedsam said, "A boy couldn't ask for much more than that."

Except maybe a family. Ezra sighed. "Yes, sir."

Colonel Friedsam nodded toward the door and Ezra hurried to open it for a man who removed his hat and muttered a greeting as he entered. After the man was out of earshot, Colonel Friedsam placed a hand upon Ezra's shoulder. "Do you know why I sought you out that day in the market?"

"Because you felt sorry for me?"

"Sorry? Now why would I feel sorry for you? Why, just the opposite; I admired your tenaciousness and your compassion. But in truth, I approached you because you reminded me of my dear cousin Benjamin, God rest his soul. Benjamin Altman is the man who had the vision for this store. He never had a family of his own, but he dreamed of owning a store where he could use the money to help others. His employees were his family and he made sure that, even after his death, his family would be taken care of."

"He's just like Angus. He always takes care of the people that live around him. Just like he took care of me and Old Granny. Then Granny died and I had to leave."

"You miss him, don't you?"

Ezra nodded his head.

"Did he tell you why you had to go?"

"He said he didn't want me to stay there after he died. He said if I didn't leave now that I would never go. He told me to go out west. But I don't know why he didn't just go and take me with him."

"Your friend is mighty old. Maybe he was afraid to do that. Maybe he thought if he took you out west and then died, you would be all alone."

Ezra hadn't thought about that. "But I'm all alone here."

"No, you're not, son. You work here, and as long as you do, you will always have a family."

But I want a real family. Ezra managed a smile and was greeted with one in return.

Colonel Friedsam pulled out his pocket watch and checked the time. "It's time for you to take your leave for the day. Make sure to go by the office and collect your weekly wage before you leave."

"Yes, sir," Ezra said in return.

"Son," Colonel Friedsam called after him.

"Yes?"

"You are not as alone as you think. I am your friend. If you ever need anything, and I do mean anything, you come to see me. If it is within my power, I will see to it. Understand?"

"Yes, sir." Ezra smiled. Only this time, the smile was genuine.

Chapter Sixteen

Sunday, August 24, 1919

"Hey, you Ezra?"

Ezra opened his eyes to see a boy standing beside his bed. Missing half his front teeth, he smiled a hapless grin when Ezra opened his eyes.

"Yes, I'm he," Ezra said, wiping the sleep from his eyes.

"They sent me to come bring ya. There's someone here to see ya," the boy replied.

Angus! Ezra hurried to dress. He scrambled from his bed, eager to see his friend. They were halfway down the hallway when he realized he'd forgotten to put on his jacket. He thought to go and retrieve it but was too eager to see his friend.

"I don't get visitors," the boy said over his shoulder.

Ezra hadn't either, until now. "I didn't know Angus was coming to see me. He never said he would."

The boy shot him a glance. "It's not a man."

"What?"

"Your visitor. She's a woman. Got a kid with her."

The only woman he knew was Mrs. Duffy. *She's come to tell me that Angus is dead.* Ezra's heart began to pound and he blew out a breath to keep from crying.

"You coming?"

Ezra looked up to see that the boy had stopped at the door to the stairs. Only then did he realize his own feet had stopped moving. Why'd she think to come and tell him such awful news? He would have preferred to never know of his friend's passing. Willing his feet to move, he pressed forward. The woman was here and there was nothing to be done about it now.

"You're new here, right?" the boy said as they descended the stairs. He'd slowed to meet Ezra's pace.

"Yes, a month so," Ezra replied.

"I'm Pete. You got a job?"

"I do," Ezra mumbled.

"Think you can get me one? A job. I'm gonna get kicked out soon if I don't pay my rent. I'm only still here because I run errands and stuff. Like coming for you."

"I suppose I could ask the Colonel," Ezra answered halfheartedly.

"Tell them I said I'd work real hard." The boy stopped at the door to the main floor. "You okay, Ezra? You don't look so good."

No, he wasn't okay. He was about to spill the contents of his stomach. "I'll do."

Ezra watched as the floor passed under his feet. The only thing keeping him moving forward was matching Pete step for step. He saw the large door to the main entrance looming in the distance and thought to start running, push through the door, and never look back.

What I am afraid to hear, I'd better say first myself. The words came in Angus' voice, understandably, as the man had said them often enough. "Angus is dead."

Pete stopped and gaped at him open mouthed. "What?"

"That's why the woman is here. She came to tell me Angus is dead."

Fear tugged at Pete's face. "Who's Angus?"

"A friend."

"Oh," the boy said nervously. "You want I should stay with you?"

"No. The hard part is over," Ezra replied. It was true; his legs were moving on their own accord and his heart rate had nearly returned to normal.

Pete, on the other hand, had turned white as a sheet and stood rooted in place. "The woman is waiting in the front office. I'll come find you later."

Ezra understood. He would be hard pressed to continue if he had another choice. He waved a hand to Pete and went to face the news. Once he reached the office, he stood staring at the doorknob. While he opened doors countless times each day, this one proved to be the most difficult. After several moments, he gathered his courage and turned the knob.

Mrs. Duffy stood at the far side of the room, staring out one of the tall windows. Her hair appeared to be freshly pinned and she wore a pale blue dress he'd never seen before. Her youngest son was at her side, pointing and jabbering at something he saw. Just as his brain registered that the boy was speaking English and wearing a dress, the woman turned to face him.

Momma! Every emotion he'd ever experienced in life slammed into him, and for a moment, he was unable to breathe. He'd thought he'd seen her so many times over the years that he knew this too to be just another cruel illusion. He closed his eyes then opened them once more, and yet she was still standing there, illuminated by the light shining in the window.

"Momma?" The word came out in a whisper.

"Yes, Ezra, it is I," she said, reaching for him. And then he was there, with her arms holding him so tight, he knew her to be real. He clung to her, afraid that if he were to let go, he would wake to find it all a wonderful dream.

"Ezra, my Ezra," she said, sobbing his name over and over, her tears wetting his cheeks as her kisses wiped them away once more.

"Momma, crying?" a small, fearful voice asked, breaking the moment.

Momma? Ezra pulled away, blinking his surprise at the girl who looked to be no older than Tobias when last he saw his brother.

His mother brushed the tears from her face and reached a hand to the child. "Eugenia, come meet your brother."

Eugenia studied him with big brown eyes, then pushed back against his mother. A flash of jealousy washed over him, catching him by surprise.

He lifted his gaze and met his mother's eyes. "I

thought you were dead."

Her eyes flew open, her head tilting as if she hadn't heard him right. "Why?"

Before he could answer, the door opened and a man stuck his head inside. "Is everything okay, Mrs. Millett?"

"Yes, thank you," his mother said and smiled.

"Take all the time you need. We'll not disturb you again," he said, motioning toward the chairs.

Ezra's heart swelled with joy at seeing his mother smile. She looked well. He tried to remember the last time he'd seen her looking so contented. *It's because Papa is dead.* He lowered his eyes in shame.

Sharon Millett settled the girl at a table and handed her a few picture books then motioned toward the chairs. "Ezra, come sit with me."

He sat across from her, his head swimming with questions. He held his tongue, waiting for her to speak.

She looked toward the girl then returned her attention to him, keeping her voice low. "Why did you think me to be dead?"

"I saw you lying on the floor. You weren't moving. Papa…" He swallowed. "I thought he had killed you."

Understanding washed over her face.

"No, we, your papa and I, had argued. We did so much back then. Anyway, I had not been feeling well. I did not know at the time that I was with child." She glanced at Eugenia and smiled. "I hadn't eaten much for a time and I passed out…went to sleep for a while."

A tear rolled down his cheek and he batted it away.

"Do you hate me, Momma?"

She frowned. "Oh, Ezra, what makes you think that?"

"Because I killed Papa," he blurted.

She opened her mouth, closed it once more, and placed a hand to her mouth. "Oh, Ezra, it's not true. Your papa's not dead."

He could not have been more surprised if she'd walked over and slapped him right in the face. "But the knife?"

"Oh, you injured him to be sure. But he is very much alive."

He started to tremble and she held her arms to him once more. He went to her, climbing onto her lap as he'd done so often when he were still a child. "He must be fearfully angry with me."

"He…we are mighty grateful to you," she said in return.

"Grateful? For hurting him?"

"Ezra, that night was a million lifetimes ago. So many things have changed since then."

"Like a new sister to take our place," he said and narrowed his eyes at the girl.

"I love your sister very much, but she could never take your place. You will know this to be true when you have children of your own someday. When I discovered you and Tobias to be gone, I wished to die." She lowered her voice. "A part of me wished…your papa was hurt and the police came. The landlord had been trying to get us out of the building for months so that he could bring in more families and charge them each for rent. He…the landlord used that to see us gone. Your papa had to stay in the hospital for nearly a week. But in that time, he did not have a drop to drink. He was so ashamed at what he'd caused you to do, and at having you and Tobias run away, that he made a promise to us all that he would never put his lips to the bottle again."

She lifted his chin so he could see her face. "You did not kill Papa; you saved him. You saved me and your sister too. Papa was getting worse by the day. If you had not done what you did, he would have killed me and the baby too."

He wondered where his papa was, but more so, it had not been lost on him that his mother had not asked about Tobias. "Tobias is gone. I looked for him but could not find him."

She closed her eyes briefly then opened them once more. "Once I was well enough to look for you boys, I went out to search for you every day. But the city is so big. I started visiting asylums around the city, leaving your names and making them promise to tell me if they found you or Tobias. I found your brother once."

Ezra pushed off her lap. "You did?"

"Almost." She nodded to the other chair and waited for him to sit. "It was about a year from the date you disappeared. They sent a messenger to tell me that he'd been sent out on a train. They thought him to be an orphan and he'd been placed with a lady."

That's one of the trains Angus told me about. He was about to say as much when she began speaking once more.

"Something had happened, and by the time they told me, your brother was on his way back to New York. I found out when he would return and went to meet the train. Only your brother decided he did not wish to be placed into the asylum. He stole from the man he was traveling with and disappeared. I've not seen or heard from him since." She was crying now. Ezra started to go to her, but she waved him off. "Eugenia was new. She'd soiled herself and was crying something fierce. So I stepped aside to tend to her. If not, maybe I would have seen him or he me. But he's gone."

"I'm sorry, Momma."

She shook her head. "None of this is your fault."

"But…"

"None of it," she said firmly.

"Momma, where is Papa?" Ezra wasn't sure if he really wanted to know, but the fact that his papa wasn't there bothered him.

His mother wiped her eyes and pulled herself taller. "Your father went out west."

"Out west? You mean he went to find Tobias?"

"No, he left even before Eugenia was born. Remember I told you he was ashamed by what he'd become?"

"Yes."

"Well, he said he was going to go away until he could

make me proud of him again."

Ezra sighed. "It didn't happen."

"Yes, yes it did. Your papa went to Nebraska to find your grandparents. They have a farm with a nice big house. They are not rich by any means and needed help to run the farm. They used to write letters begging us to come, saying they had plenty of room and would love to meet their grandchildren. Papa always refused, insisting he would rather make it on his own. He wrote to them, told them of his need, and they agreed to allow him to come. He's been working on their farm and he's quit the drink."

"Papa told me he couldn't give it up. I asked him to, but he told me it would find him again," Ezra sneered.

"He was wrong. I'm not just taking your papa's word for it. Your grandparents have sent me letters. It's true, Ezra. I promise you it is." Her eyebrows knitted together, and she looked as if she were about to cry once more.

"What is it, Momma?"

"I didn't know I was going to find you. I wanted to, but I didn't think I ever would."

"But you did, Momma. I'm right here."

She put up a hand to silence him. "I know. But I didn't think I would. I was to leave this Tuesday. Eugenia and I were to leave on the train and go to Papa."

Ezra wasn't sure what to say. He'd been sure she was dead and now he'd found her and she was leaving. "I'll go with you."

Her face screwed up and the tears streamed down her

face once more. "I don't have the money to bring you with me. Your papa has been working so hard. He has sent me enough money to live, but there has not been enough to pay for our trip. The Children's Aid Society is paying for me and your sister to go. I'm not sure if there is enough time to ask them to send you along too. I won't go! Not now. Not after finding you. I'll wait until we can all go together. That is, if you wish to go with us."

Of course he would.

Eugenia approached their mother and placed her hand against her cheek. "You sad, Momma?"

"No, honey, Momma is very happy."

"You don't look happy." She pouted.

Eugenia was right. Gone was the smile that lit her face when he first saw her. He turned to his mother, his words tasting like bile upon his tongue. "I want you to go. When I make enough money I will come find you."

"No," she said, shaking her head furiously. "I lost you once. I'll not risk that again. I will stay."

Ezra wanted to object, to tell her he was a man now and that he would be okay. But seeing her again stripped him of his bravado. "I'll get my things."

She shook her head, her lips quivering as she tried to find her words. "I'll not go, but you will have to stay here."

"But..."

"There's no room, Ezra. Eugenia and I are sleeping on the floor in an apartment with three other families." She pushed her tears away with trembling fingers.

"There isn't room for any more, not even a small boy."

"I have a job, Momma. I'll save all my money. It won't take long." The thought of his mother sleeping on the floor tore at his heart, but the thought of her going away was much too much to bear. While he knew he should convince her to go, he remained silent. He'd lost her once; he couldn't bear losing her again.

Chapter Seventeen

Ezra waited for his mother and sister to leave before approaching the man who oversaw the building, telling him he was taking his leave and requesting the return of his money. If his mother were not to sleep on a bed, neither would he. Besides, he could save money by not sleeping in the Lodging House. He went upstairs to collect his things, pausing when he saw the green jacket lying across the end of his bed. He thought of what Angus had said about the jacket being lucky and wondered if it was the reason his mother had found him.

He pulled it on, stuffing the paper his mother had given him with her address in the pocket for safe keeping. He'd been surprised to find she was living in an apartment in the same building as they once lived and wondered if she had been there the day he'd returned. She'd told him she had often gone to the market in search of him and his brother, leaving him to wonder if it were really his mother he had seen, only to have her disappear into the crowd. It didn't matter anymore. The ache in his heart was less than it had been in a long while, and one day soon, he hoped it to be gone altogether. He collected the pillowcase with his belongings and left.

***

Not having anywhere else to go, Ezra spent the night huddled near the door of the Altman building. He was still there when Colonel Friedsam clicked the lock the following morning.

"What's this?" he asked, frowning at Ezra.

"I'm ready to come to work, sir," Ezra said.

"Yes, I see that. Did you sleep here?"

"Yes, sir," Ezra said, pulling to his feet.

"I thought you were staying at the Lodging House."

"Oh, I was, but I'm done with that, beings I need to save my money and all."

"Have you eaten a morning meal?" he asked when Ezra's stomach rumbled.

"No, sir, nor supper either. As I said, I'm saving my money."

"Maybe you should come inside so we can have ourselves a chat," Colonel Friedsam said, holding the door for him.

Ezra followed him inside, surprised when the Colonel bypassed his office, leading the way to the employee dining room instead.

Ezra stopped at the entrance. "If it's all the same with you, sir, I'll wait out here. My stomach's mighty sore and won't be so happy if I have to watch you eat."

"You'll follow me. I shall pay for your meal," the Colonel said when Ezra hesitated yet again.

Ezra followed him inside. He didn't see any reason not to, since Colonel Friedsam had offered to pay and all.

The Colonel ordered them each a plate of fried chicken along with biscuits and gravy before lacing his fingers together and ordering Ezra to tell him what was amiss.

"My momma, she found me. She didn't think she would, so she was supposed to go out on a train tomorrow with my new little sister. Only now she's not going." Ezra lowered his eyes. "I know I should have told her to go, on account of the people were going to pay for her trip and all, but I was afraid I'd never see her again."

"Wait, I thought you said your parents were dead. You're telling me your mother is alive?"

"Yes, sir and my papa too. I thought I'd killed him, but she said it wasn't so. I believe her and all 'cause my momma, she don't lie."

Colonel Friedsam leaned back in his chair as a woman approached the table with a tray that held small dishes of food. He waited for her to leave and for Ezra to fill his plate before speaking. "Perhaps you should start from the beginning."

"I did. My momma found me," Ezra said, tearing into the chicken.

"No, the other beginning. The one where you thought your momma to be dead, and let's not forget the part where you thought you'd killed your papa," Colonel Friedsam said, spooning gravy onto his biscuits.

Ezra was hungry, so he ate while telling the events over the last four years, grateful the man didn't feel the need to correct him for speaking with his mouthful. He told him about his time with Angus, even though he'd already told the man a little about that before.

"What about you? Do you think your papa has given up the drink?" he asked when Ezra finished.

"I've thought about that some, and if my grandparents think it to be true, then so do I."

"You've said you have never met your grandparents. What makes you think you can trust them?"

"On account of they're old."

Colonel Friedsam, who had been in the process of taking a drink of his coffee, coughed into his cup.

"Are you okay?" Ezra asked when he continued to cough.

"Yes, quite. It just went down the wrong way. So, it has been your experience that old people don't lie."

"Oh, yes, sir. Angus, he thinks my grandparents are Irish. They would have come over on a ship round the same time he did, and he never lied to me. He told me from the beginning that when Granny died, I'd have to go. I didn't like it much, but I knew it to be true 'cause he told me so."

"Ah, to be young and innocent," the Colonel said, lifting his cup once again.

"Yes, sir," Ezra said and the Colonel laughed.

"When was your mother supposed to go on the train?"

"Tomorrow morning," Ezra said.

Colonel Friedsam pulled his watch from his pocket and studied it for a moment. "I guess we have some work to do."

"Yes, sir. I need to earn some money." Ezra replied, bobbing his head in agreement.

"No, I don't suppose you'll be working here any longer," the Colonel said, rising from his chair.

Ezra leaped to his feet. "But I got to work. I got to make enough money so we can go be with Papa."

"Your momma and sister will be on that train tomorrow." He put up a hand to silence Ezra's objections. "Don't you worry, son. I'll see to it you're right there with them. You go collect your momma and sister. Bring them back here and I'll see to my letter of recommendation."

"You'd do that for me?" Ezra asked, staring at the man in disbelief. "Why?"

"The same reason that you once thought to spend your money on that apron, son. If someone is in need and you can help, it makes you feel good right here," Colonel Friedsam said, tapping him softly on the chest. "That is why you bought the apron, the reason your friend Angus helps those around him, and the reason I'm going to help you now."

Ezra sighed. He was going to leave and he'd truly never see his friend again. "I wish I could tell Angus about finding my momma."

"Don't you worry about that. I will see to it he knows," Colonel Friedsam promised.

"How will you know where to find him?"

The Colonel considered his question for a moment.

"Angus made me promise to keep an eye on you and tell him if ever you needed anything."

"He did?"

"He cares about you very much. He gave you his lucky jacket, didn't he? Now, if it hasn't brought you luck, then I don't know what luck is."

Ezra looked down at the green coat. "Do you think the jacket helped me find my momma?"

"Did you find her before you had it?"

"No, sir."

"Then I think you just got your answer."

Ezra smiled. He liked thinking the jacket had something to do with him finding his mother, as that would also mean that Angus had helped as well. He paused, looking up at Colonel Friedsam once more. "Sir, you'll be needing a new doorman, right?"

"I suppose I will at that."

"There is a boy named Pete at the Lodging House. He needs a job so he can pay for his rent."

"Thank you, Ezra. I'll see he doesn't end up on the street," the Colonel assured him.

Ezra gathered the pillowcase. Angus and Colonel Friedsam were right. It felt good helping people.

***

Tuesday, August 26, 1919

Ezra stood in line beside his mother, waiting with a large group of others to be led to the train. Eugenia stood on the other side, spinning in circles, giggling as the skirt of her dress floated against the wind. His mother looked

146

at him, her eyes sparkling nearly as much as the fancy clip that held her hair in place.

His heart swelled, even though he had nothing to do with how pretty she looked. He'd collected both his mother and sister and taken them back to the store as Colonel Friedsam had directed. When they'd arrived, the Colonel had a staff waiting, tasked with helping them each find a new set of clothes for the trip. His mother had balked, but Colonel Friedsam had insisted he was only doing his duty, further insisting that everyone who rode the trains was given a new outfit prior to their departure. When Ezra had questioned him about his remark in private, the man had admitted to stretching the truth a tad, saying that while everyone received a new set of travel clothes, not everyone got the privilege of choosing their own. Nor were they given an extra set and told to discard the rags they'd been wearing. While Ezra had received two new sets of clothes, he'd opted to keep the jacket Angus had given him. While his mother had raised an eyebrow at seeing him in his fine clothes and oversized green jacket, she'd kept her comments to herself.

"Thank you, Ezra," she said for the hundredth time.

"It wasn't me, Momma," he repeated as he had each time before.

"You're wrong, Ezra. You may not have given us these beautiful clothes, but it is because of you that all of this is happening. Your papa needed help. You made him open his eyes."

"Oh, Momma. I never meant to hurt him. I don't even know how it happened. What if he…"

"Ezra, I know you're worried, but I've spoken to your papa. He's a changed man. You believe me, don't you?"

"Angus told me about the man he used to work for and how he'd taken to the drink and would beat him something awful. He said the man quit the drink and was nice again. He's the one who gave Angus this jacket. I guess if he can get better, then so can Papa."

His mother blew out a sigh and he wondered if she'd been worried all along.

"Momma, if Papa ever turns to the drink again, I'll not stay," Ezra said firmly.

She looked at him, then gazed at Eugenia, who'd tired of playing with her dress and was clacking her new shoes against the tiled floors of the depot. "Neither will I, Ezra, neither will I."

She'd no sooner said the words when the lady in charge waved her arms to gather the group together.

"We'll be boarding the train soon. Make sure you all have your boarding passes. We'll all be traveling together for the first part of the trip, however, since we all have different destinations, most will be changing trains along the way. On behalf of The Children's Aid Society who has made arrangements for you and your families to go out in search of a better life, I'd like to take a moment and wish you all the best in your endeavors. Now, if you'll all follow me, it is time to begin our journey."

Ezra stayed by his mother's side as they walked through the doors and gawked with the others as they approached the massive train. Eugenia lost all interest in her clothing and stared open-mouthed at the mountain of steel idling before them. As they stood waiting to board, she bit her bottom lip and looked as if she were about to cry.

Ezra took her by the hand and smiled. To his surprise, she looked up at him, her large brown eyes filled with adoration. It had been a long time since he'd felt this content. His only regret was that his brother was not going with them.

His mother climbed onto the steps and hesitated, casting a longing look over her shoulder, and he wondered if she too were thinking the same thing.

***

Rain pelted against the window of the train car as they neared their final destination. His mother stared out the window. She'd grown quiet after they'd switched onto the train that would carry them into Nebraska and on to the town of North Platte, where they were to meet his papa.

"It's hot, Momma," Eugenia whined.

"That it is," his mother agreed. She turned from the window. "I wish we could open the window. Don't worry, daughter; it won't be much longer until we arrive. Are you excited to finally meet your papa?"

"Yes, Momma," she said, climbing onto her lap.

"It's much too hot to have you in my lap." His mother slid over and settled the girl beside her. She turned to him and frowned. "What is it, Ezra?"

"I just realized Sister has never met Papa."

"No, she has had me all to herself all her years." She lowered her voice. "Does that bother you?"

A little. "Not much," he replied.

"She has been fortunate in her short life. While we've had our share of hardships, she will not know the horrors of the rest of the family. She sees this all as a grand adventure. We know it to be more." His mother took his hand in hers. "Ezra, I cannot promise you that life will be perfect, but I can promise it will be better than before."

"Look, Momma, buildings!" Eugenia said, pointing out the window.

Ezra stretched his neck to see through the sheets of rain. Sure enough, after seeing nothing but wide open fields most of the morning, there was a small town looming in the distance.

His mother looked out the window and giggled nervously. "Papa said it was a small town. He didn't lie."

"Angus said small towns are the best," Ezra assured her. "That's why he wanted me to go out west. He said the air smells better in small towns."

"Well, it's hotter, that's for sure," his mother replied. She fidgeted with her hair as the train rumbled to a stop.

A small crowd stood braving the rain. Ezra tried to catch a glimpse of his papa, but the water-soaked window did not allow for a clear view. To his surprise, his mother did not appear to be in a great hurry to exit the train, waiting instead until long after the other passengers departed. While Eugenia wasn't pleased, he was content to bide his time until his mother was ready.

The train whistle blared, indicating the train would soon be departing.

"Momma," Ezra said softly. "It's time to go."

His words pulled her out of her fog. She stood, tugged at her dress briefly, then picked up her umbrella and walked to the door without a word. Eugenia followed and Ezra grabbed their bag, trailing behind. The crowd had dispersed. All but one man, standing alone while the rain poured over the brim of his hat.

"Papa," Ezra whispered. He watched as his mother slowly made her way to the man who gathered her into his arms, holding her as if he meant to squeeze all the air from her body.

Eugenia stood frozen in her tracks, oblivious to the rain.

"Come along, Sister; it's right time you meet your papa." Ezra took hold of her hand, leading her to where their parents stood.

Ezra's heart drummed in his chest as his father looked him up and down. "It's good to see you, son. You've grown."

"Yes, sir," Ezra replied.

"I thank you for seeing your mother and sister here safe." His father extended his hand.

Ezra stared at the hand, which was steady despite the rain. He reached for it, and his father smiled. Releasing his hand, Papa turned his attention to Eugenia, whose dress now clung to her small frame. He opened his arms to the girl, and Ezra gave her a gentle nudge. She took a timid step then another before being hoisted into her father's arms.

"Why, aren't you the prettiest thing. You're the spitting image of your momma," Papa said, wiping the water from her face. "What say we get you all in out of the rain?"

Ezra picked up the small case that held all their possessions and followed as he led them across the street to a small buggy with a canopy and two bench seats. A man sat on the front seat and tipped his hat to his mother. The man turned his head toward him and smiled a wrinkled grin. A lump formed in Ezra's throat. For a moment, he thought the man to be Angus.

The man looked toward the sky and laughed a hearty laugh. "It be a fine day for young ducks."

"That's my da's way of telling you what you already know," Papa said as he helped Momma into the back of the buggy. "We'll make the introductions after we get in out of the rain."

"And just what is that?" Momma asked as he hoisted Eugenia up beside her.

"He's telling ye it's raining," Ezra said, grinning at the man.

"Aye, I'm pleased to see the lad knows a thing about

his heritage." He patted the seat beside him. "Climb up here next to ye gramps so we can have ourselves a proper chat."

Ezra looked to his papa for permission.

"Go on, son. I'm going to sit in the back with your momma and sister."

Ezra climbed onto the seat, trembling at the familiarity of the situation.

His grandfather pulled on the reins and clicked his tongue to get the horse moving. Leaning closer, the man elbowed him and offered him the reins. "Want to give it a go, lad?"

"Doesn't she know the way?"

"Oc' no. She's but a wee lass no older than that little one in the back seat," he said, shaking his head.

"So she's not going to die anytime soon?"

"That mare is just getting started in life," his grandfather assured him. "She and I will be with this family a long time to come. Now give the reins a shake and tell her to get along. Your Granny's been at the stove cooking all day. She'll be eager to see ye home. She's been wishing for a family for a long time, doncha know."

Ezra pulled his jacket tight against the rain that drifted in the sides of the wagon and sighed a contented sigh. Yes, he did know.

Epilogue

"Ezra, please take that jacket off. It's over a hundred degrees out," his mother said, fanning her face with a newspaper.

"I'm not hot," Ezra lied.

She wrinkled her nose. "At least take it off so that I can wash it. Why, it's so dirty, it could stand on its own."

"But, Momma, Angus said I must take care of it."

"Indeed. You're doing your friend a disservice by keeping it that way. Now take it off. You can have it back when it's clean."

Ezra hesitated, then shrugged out of the coat and handed it to his momma, who held it with the tips of her fingers. She picked up the scrub brush and used it to gently brush the outer layer. "It's a rather peculiar color for a coat, don't you think?"

Ezra smiled, remembering the first time he saw the man wearing it. "It made Angus look like a leprechaun."

"I can see why." She lifted the sleeve and began running the brush down the length of the arm, frowning when she reached the pit of the arm. Lowering the brush, she felt the fabric with her fingers. "Ezra, does the jacket bother your arm when you wear it?"

It did, though he hadn't wished to tell her so. "A little."

"Why didn't you say anything?"

"I was afraid you'd make me take it off."

She clicked her tongue. "Ezra, you've been on your own long enough. I think you can make your own decisions about what you'll wear or not wear. If you'll allow me, though, I'd like to take a closer look at this and see if I can fix it so it won't be so uncomfortable. Would that be all right with you?"

Ezra nodded his head.

"Bring me my sewing box."

Ezra hurried to retrieve the small box that held her needle and thread along with a few buttons and a sturdy pair of scissors.

"You're blocking the light," she fussed when he hovered over her.

He backed off but kept the jacket in his sight as she turned it inside out and carefully snipped the thread that covered the hole. When she'd finished removing the stitching, she wrinkled her brow.

"Ezra, look here. This is not a hole, but a hidden pocket that's been sewn shut." She pushed two fingers in the pocket and pulled out a satin pouch, which was closed together with a simple drawstring. She started to pull open the pouch then handed it to Ezra instead.

He pulled the strings apart and gasped.

"Well, what is it?" his mother asked.

He reached into the pouch and pulled out a stack of money, folded in half and held together with a piece of paper and a money clip. He handed it to his mother.

"How much is it, Momma?"

She slid the bills from one hand to another, her mouth moving as she counted. When she finished, her face was a brilliant shade of pink. "Ezra, did you not know about this?"

"No, Momma," he said, shaking his head. "Is it a lot of money?"

"Yes, Ezra. It is more money than I have ever seen at one time."

"How much," he repeated.

"Four hundred and eighty-nine dollars."

"Is that enough to buy a plot of land?"

"Why, yes, I suppose it is. Where did you hear that from?"

"Angus told me I shouldn't take the jacket off until I had enough money to buy a plot of land. The jacket is rather hot, so I thought maybe I have enough."

She smiled and placed the money back in the clip then unfolded the paper. "It's a letter from your friend Angus."

"What's it say?"

"Lad,

"If you are reading this, you've found my gift to you. I gave it the same way it was given to me so many years ago. I hope ye shall put it to good use and buy yourself a chance for a better life. Remember the lessons I've taught ye and as ye go about life know this:

"You can accomplish more with a kind word and a shillelagh than you can with just a kind word. Find your way in the world and be kind to others in your path and you will serve this old man proud. It was good knowing you.

"Your friend,

"Angus."

When his mother finished reading, she had tears in her eyes.

"Wait until Papa sees this," Ezra said once she'd finished.

His mother shook his head. "How about we keep this to ourselves for now."

"You mean keep a secret from Papa?"

"Not just Papa, everyone."

"But…"

"No, hear me out. I think your friend Angus would approve. If he wanted everyone to know about your money, he would have just given it to you. He didn't, did he?"

"No, ma'am."

"That's right. He hid it in your jacket to keep it safe. So what do you say we put it back to keep it safe?"

"You mean I have to keep wearing it?"

"Only if you want to. But I think Angus would be happy that you know where it is. We can hang the jacket in your closet, and you will always know where to find it if you need it. How would that be?"

"What if someone steals my jacket?"

His mother ran a hand over the well-worn fabric. "I don't think we have to worry about that."

Ezra stood watch as his mother returned the money to the hidden pocket and sewed a simple stitch to hold it together. When she was finished, she handed him the jacket and picked at the threads that littered the blue apron he'd purchased with the money he'd earned from working at the department store. It was still clean, as Granny insisted on doing the cooking, leaving his mother time to teach him and his sister their lessons each day.

The front door creaked opened. Ezra looked up to see his papa standing in the doorway. His father looked in his direction and smiled an easy smile. "Grampa and I are going fishing down at the pond. Want to come?"

"Sure! Let me just put my jacket in my room." Ezra raced up the stairs to his room and hung the jacket on a hook inside his closet. As he neared the bottom of the stairs, he saw his parents standing in the middle of the room, his father's arms wrapped securely around his mother. Her head lay against his shoulder, eyes closed as his papa whispered something Ezra could not hear. She opened her eyes, saw him watching, and closed them once again.

Not wishing to interrupt, Ezra sat on the step and sighed a contented sigh. His mother was happy. His father sober, and for the first time in as long as he could remember, he didn't have to worry about going to bed hungry. He wasn't sure if it was because Angus had given him the jacket or if he really possessed the luck of the Irish, but he liked to think it a bit of both.

The End...

Continue the journey with Sherry A. Burton's The Orphan Train Saga.

Please see the excerpt from Shameless, *Book 2 of the Orphan Train Saga, at the end of this book.*

Historical Note...

The story you just read highlights the fact that family units were sent west on trains along with orphan and homeless children. Though I'd heard a bit about it before, I hadn't done much by way of research on the family emigration program. Before beginning this book, I contacted Lori Halfhide – head researcher at the National Orphan Train Complex in Concordia, Kansas – to tell her of my plan to showcase the family emigration program. Lori was kind enough to send me an article along with newspaper clippings that told of families being sent out on the trains. In some cases, only mothers with children were sent out to family members waiting to welcome them to their new lives. In others, the articles show the entire family unit being sent west in search of greater opportunities. I am grateful that reporters took the time to document so many cases of families being sent west, printing a brief history of the family's struggle to make it in the big city and further validate their need for help.

It is clear that The Children's Aid Society were not monsters trying to steal children from their families. On the contrary, they had programs in place aimed at helping families remain together, thereby preserving the family unit. In some cases, the families were responsible for paying half the fare, in other cases – if the family had minor children who would benefit greatly from being removed from the city and sent west – the CAS would pay for the entire cost of the trip.

Trivia

I used Ezra to tell this story as many of my readers have written, wishing to know what happened to him. I used the "vegetable man" for the backdrop as one of the articles I read told of a boy who'd worked for a vegetable vendor until the man's horse died and left them both without a job.

A special thanks to:

My editor, Beth, for allowing me to keep my voice.

My cover artist and media design guru, Laura Prevost, thanks for keeping me current.

My proofreader, Latisha Rich, for that extra set of eyes.

To my amazing team of beta readers, thank you for helping take a final look.

To my husband, thank you for your endless hours of researching, your help with all things genealogy, and for allowing me to bounce story ideas off of you.

Please find it in your heart to take a moment and go to Amazon to leave a review. Reviews are also welcomed at Barnes & Noble, Bookbub, and Goodreads as well. If you purchased the book at a signing or from my website, please begin your review by including that information. If not, Amazon may not allow the review.

Most importantly, please tell EVERYONE and share in the reading groups! As an indie author, word of mouth is the best publicity I can get.
Thank you for taking this journey with me.

Sherry A. Burton

Please remember to follow me on social media and sign up for my newsletter on my website to keep up to date with all new releases.

For more information on the author and her works, please see www.SherryABurton.com
Follow Sherry on social media:
https://www.facebook.com/SherryABurtonauthor
https://www.amazon.com/Sherry-A.-Burton/e/B005PM6QFG?ref=dbs_m_mng_rwt_auth
https://www.bookbub.com/profile/sherry-a-burton
https://www.instagram.com/authorsherryaburton

About the Author

Born in Kentucky, Sherry married a Navy man at the age of eighteen. She and her now-retired Navy husband have three children and ten grandchildren.

After moving around the country and living in nine different states, Sherry and her husband now live in Michigan's thumb, with their three rescue cats and a standard poodle named Murdoc.

Sherry writes full time and is currently hard at work on the next novel in her Orphan Train Saga, an eighteen-book historical fiction series that revolves around the orphan trains.

When Sherry is not writing, she enjoys traveling to lectures and signing events, where she shares her books and speaks about the history of the Orphan Trains.

Excerpt from Shameless (Tobias' Story)

Tobias ran from the building and was instantly met with darkness. However, it wasn't the darkness that frightened him, but the thick blanket of fog that hovered in the air. A damp netting surrounded him as he rushed out into the night. In his haste, he forgot to turn and veered just before running into the tall brick building he'd not been able to see only seconds before. He slowed his pace but continued to move forward, frightened not only of the fog but of inhabitants that could be heard but not seen. The fog reminded him of the steam that rose from the many vents in the city. Only the fog was everywhere, and he could not run through it to get to the other side. He heard voices drifting about the fog and trembled. He'd seen fog before, but he'd never had to face it alone. Still, he was more afraid of what his papa would do to him if he caught up with him, so he kept moving forward. He thought he was lost but then realized instinct had taken him to where he often traveled with his mother and his brother. As he remembered his brother's words, a tear slid down his cheek. He didn't want to believe that his momma was dead, but if Ezra said it was true, he believed him. Ezra didn't lie. An image of his brother came to mind, replaying the way the knife Ezra had slid into his papa's belly easier than it had torn through the hardened hunk of cheese. Without warning, his stomach lurched, sending its contents flying. The single tear was replaced by a steady stream.

He spit to clear the vile taste from his mouth, wiped at his nose with the end of the pillowcase, and cursed at the tears that continued to fall. He half-expected to feel a hand strike a blow as the words slipped past his trembling lips. When nothing happened, he repeated the words and added a few more for good measure. The tears ebbed as he felt empowered by the toxicity of the forbidden words.

Somehow he made his way to where the vendor carts were supposed to be, but the street was mostly empty. Behind him, a man's voice bellowed in the distance. Fear propelled him forward. He saw a shadowy shape and squinted to see past the fog. He caught sight of a wagon and sighed. There were no horses attached, but as he neared, he saw the wagon was surrounded by bales of hay. He pulled at a bale until he had an opening large enough to squeeze through then ducked under, intending to hide until the fog lifted. The moment he stopped, he knew he was not alone. The smell of sweat and unwashed bodies invaded his nostrils. He tried to stay quiet, but fear won out as he felt fingers grasp hold of his leg. He screamed, and the hand let go of the leg, covering his mouth instead.

"Silence that yap of yours before you get us all tossed in jail with the murderers and rapists." The voice was firm but seemed more concerned than angry.

Tobias squelched his fear and nodded his agreement. He breathed a sigh of relief when the hand lifted.

"You are welcome to stay under here if you can remain quiet. The night is much too dangerous to roam the streets. With fog this thick, we wouldn't be able to see anyone until they were right upon us. What is your name, boy? You are a boy, right?"

Of course he was a boy, but then the voice would not know that, as it was too dark to see. "Yes, I'm a boy."

"Your name, then?" the voice said when Tobias hesitated.

"Mouse." Of course it was not his real name, but he didn't know who was asking and was afraid if he told his real name, they would take him back to his papa.

"Better a mouse than a rat," the voice said in reply.

Tobias waited for further conversation, but there was none. As he sat there, he felt his eyes grow heavy until exhaustion won and he drifted into an uneasy sleep. Sometime later, the dreams began. He ran through the fog calling for his sister. "Anastasia! Where are you? I know you are out here somewhere. I don't know what has happened to the family. Papa is mad, and I can't go home." A muffled voice called his name. Not the one his parents bestowed upon him, but the one given to him by his sister. Mouse.

"Yo, Mouse, time to get moving," the voice called

more urgently.

Tobias opened his eyes, blinking to orient himself. Daylight drifted in through the cracks between the hay bales as the mixture of damp hay and unwashed bodies pulled at his senses. Suddenly, the events of the previous evening came flooding back. Instantly, he was fully awake, crouched on his heels and ready to bolt.

"Didn't I tell you the boy has some grit?"

Tobias recognized the voice from the previous evening. Turning, he could just make out the face that went with it. The boy looked to be several years older than he. Although his hair was neatly cut, that was the only thing neat about him. Shadows surrounded the boy's eyes, his clothes hung from his body in tattered shreds, and he emitted a smell bad enough to make a five-year-old take notice. He was just about to mention the odor when a second voice drew his attention. He turned to his left and saw another boy he hadn't realized was there.

"He's quick on his feet, but that doesn't mean we should let him in. He's just a kid," the second boy sneered.

The first boy laughed. "So were you when I brought you in."

The second boy snorted. "We're the same age."

"Yes, but we're older now and wiser. Besides, the kid would be a great distraction."

Tobias wasn't sure what was going on, but something told him to remain quiet until things were settled.

The boy to his left was just as grubby as the first, and when he spoke, Tobias could see he was missing several teeth. The boy tilted his head in his direction and Tobias was shocked to see he was also missing a good chunk of his left ear. Tobias gasped and the boy lifted a hand to his ear.

"What happened to your ear?" Tobias whispered.

The first boy laughed. "Chunk got into a fight with one of the Gas House Gang. Chunk belted him a good one, so the boy got mad and bit off a chunk of his ear. That's how he got the name Chunk."

Tobias blinked and stared at Chunk in wide-eyed wonder. "Can he still hear?"

"Why are you asking him? Of course I can hear. People don't hear with their ears; they hear with the hole in their ears."

The first boy rocked back on his heels "Go easy on the kid, Chunk. A thing like that takes a bit of getting used to. Why, I nearly pissed myself the first time I saw ya."

"Oh yeah, well, why don't you tell him how you got your name, Lucky."

Tobias turned towards the boy who had allowed him to stay.

Lucky held up his hand to show the first two fingers were missing all the way down to the palm. Nary so much as a stub remained to show if they'd even ever been there. The hand appeared to be long healed, as Lucky smiled and tapped his two remaining fingers to his thumb.

Tobias studied the hand with a mixture of fear and awe. He'd seen men with missing legs and arms standing on the street and asking for money. His momma told him they got injured in the war and that the doctors had to cut off their limbs. He didn't know what a war was, but he remembered being scared he would end up in one. He'd been afraid to go to sleep that night. When his momma asked him why, he said that without a leg, he wouldn't be able to run away when his papa was mad. Without arms, he wouldn't be able to hug her before he went to bed at night. She'd pulled him close and told him she hoped he would never have to go to war either. He shook off the memory and pointed at Lucky's hand. "Did the doctors cut your fingers off?"

Lucky shook his head. "No, the law took my fingers for stealing."

Tobias swallowed. "How come you call yourself Lucky if they cut your fingers off?" "Because they wanted to cut off my whole hand. Instead, they cut these two off to teach me a lesson."

"Did it work? Did it teach you not to steal?"

"No, but it did teach me not to get caught," Lucky said, and both he and Chunk burst out laughing.

There was a rustling sound as one of the hay bales slid from beneath the wagon, allowing light to flood in. The shadow of a man appeared in the opening. "You boys come on out of there." Lucky and Chunk scrambled through the opening. Tobias hesitated before grabbing hold of his pillowcase and following. As he crawled through the opening, he noticed the street once more filled with wagons. Some had slipped into their spots for the day; others waited in line, ready to park and sell their offerings. He was relieved to see the thick fog had mostly lifted, the damp streets quickly growing dry via the bright rays of morning sun. Men laughed and joked as they greeted one another, a scene he'd seen so many times when he visited Market Street with his mother. While she was not with him, the scene was momentarily comforting.

The second he breached the opening, rough hands latched on to his collar, lifting him so that his toes barely touched the ground.

"Who do we have here?" The words came out in a growl flowing past in a haze of cigar smoke.

"The kid's name is Mouse. He rolled in with the fog last night. The poor sap was scared out of his wits, so we let him stay," Lucky offered.

The man scowled at the boy. "You know the rules, Lucky. It's five cents a night to sleep under the wagon. What do you say, kid? Got any dough?"

Tobias shook his head in reply.

"What about you, Lucky? You allowed him to stay. Are you going to cough up the nickel?"

Lucky pulled out his pockets to show his lack of funds and shrugged.

The man snatched the pillowcase from Tobias' hand

and released his hold on his collar, causing him to land in a heap at his feet. "What's in the sack, boy?"

Before he could reply, the man dumped the contents onto the dirt. The scowl on the man's face must have matched his own, as the man laughed and placed a heavy foot onto the pile of clothes, twisting them further into the dirt. Tobias pictured his mother standing in front of the kitchen sink, rubbing the family's laundry across the rough washboard until the knuckles of her fingers bled. As he pictured his momma, he remembered Ezra's words, Papa killed Momma, and something inside him snapped. He lunged forward, wrapping his arms around the man's leg. Opening his mouth, he latched on to his thigh, biting for all he was worth. The man yelled, sputtering vile words and shaking his leg. Tobias tightened his grip, burying his teeth deeper. The man's voice pitched higher, screaming for someone to kill the varmint. He felt the blood seep into his mouth as two sets of hands managed to separate him, tossing him backward. He scrambled to his feet, wiped the blood from his face, and glared at the man.

"That boy is an animal," the man screamed, pointing a shaky finger at Tobias. "I'll have him thrown in the jail with the rest of the crazies. The two of you too!" he shouted at both Lucky and Chunk.

The boys rushed to where Tobias stood. Each hooked an arm through his and kept running, dragging him backwards. Tobias wanted to shout at them to stop so that he could return and retrieve his discarded clothing but decided against it. Now that he was calm, the clothing didn't seem worth the trouble. Instead, he lifted his legs and waited to see where the boys were taking him. He didn't have to wait long as they veered into an alley and released him.

"I saw a dog act like that once, and the farmer had to stab him with a pitchfork," Chunk said breathlessly. "Are you mad, Mouse?"

"I'm not mad at anyone," Tobias said, shaking his head. "I think that man might be mad, though. He sure sounded mad."

Chunk blinked, staring at him open-mouthed.

Lucky bent and peered into his eyes. "Are you okay, kid? What came over you? Why did you bite that guy like that?"

Tobias shrugged. "He reminded me of my dad."

Lucky studied him for a good minute without saying a word. Finally, he stood and nodded his head. "I get that, Mouse. I really do. I've wanted to tear into my pops a time or two."

Tobias felt his stomach rumble. "I'm kinda hungry. Ezra cut a hunk of cheese, but Papa caught him."

"Ezra?"

"My brother," Tobias said and felt his eyes grow misty as he told the boys of the events that led him to the streets.

"Not to worry, kid," Lucky said when he finished. "Chunk and I are your brothers now. Ain't that right, Chunk?"

"Brothers," Chunk agreed. "But I think you need a better name than Mouse."

"We could call you Chomps or Chops," Lucky agreed.

"If it's all the same, I prefer Mouse," Tobias said. He wanted to add that his sister gave him the name, but he was feeling rather emotional. He'd already shed a few tears, and the last thing he wanted was to have his new friends think he was a crybaby. A reputation like that would be hard to live down.

"Mouse it is, then," Lucky said, clapping him on the back. "Have you ever dipped pockets before?"

Tobias shrugged. "I don't know what that means."

"Then you probably haven't done it. Have you ever taken anything that didn't belong to you?"

Tobias felt his face flush. He'd been stealing apples the day Anastasia disappeared. He couldn't help but think he was responsible for her disappearance.

The boys burst out laughing.

"Ha, from the look on your face I would say that you have. You don't have to be embarrassed around us. You just have to be good at what you do. That's where we come in. Stick with us, and we'll show you how it's done. Just make sure you do exactly as I say so you don't end up like me," Lucky said and waved his defective hand in front of Tobias.

From the author…If you've enjoyed what you just read, continue the journey with the other books in The

Orphan Train Saga. Remember to begin the journey with Discovery and read the books in order. https://www.amazon.com/dp/B07KK42KZ1

www.ingramcontent.com/pod-product-compliance
Lightning Source LLC
Chambersburg PA
CBHW062309200726
48292CB00004BA/1492